LAST
BANK
HOLIDAY

CHRISTINA DELMONTE

To Rob, Sam and Sacha

Dedicated to my Mum,
who sadly suffered from
Alzheimer's.

For information on Alzheimer's contact
alzheimersresearchuk.org
alz.org

I would like to thank my editor,
Sian-Elin Flint-Freel

Zane Lewis Knutsford
Shirley's Nails Knutsford
The Hollies Tarporley for the front cover image

Prologue

The sky is deep blue and the rays make my eyes stream; it's a struggle to keep them open. Sharp grains of sand whip the side of my face and my limbs are contorted in an odd position. Weirdly, my left side is numbed cold and stone-like, whilst my right side swelters in this mid-day sun. I seriously need painkillers and my head is splitting. It's too late in the day for a hangover.

Gulls squeal like sirens and lightning streaks across the sky, which only adds to my confusion. What's happening?

In the pit of my stomach there's a feeling of impending doom.

I call you for some tablets but you're all chasing the waves and totally oblivious. Your screams pierce through me, increasing my pain. There's a tall, dark shadow behind you. You're arguing. I rub my eyes to focus. You look like you're being dragged away by some random stranger. There's nothing I can do. He has you, he has them, and he has a gun!

"Shit, it's him... Karen! Get away from my kids... Run, Karen!" I try to scream but instead it's a muffled slur that babbles from my mouth.

"You sick bastard, leave them alone!" Again, I try, but only confused garble leaves my lips.

Then, there's voices, from nowhere:

"Will, baby, stay with me."

"Son, wake up."

"Dad?... Stop shaking me, you're making my head worse."

The loud voices rip through me. I clamp my temples with my fists to try to control this agony.

The sky still flashes blue. The sirens keep screeching. My head is excruciating. My family are dragged away.

1

Karen

Sunday May bank Holiday 10am

They've told me to keep talking to you, to say anything. That according to research, you are still able to hear. So I whisper that we love you, beg you to wake, to come back to us, just to open your eyes. I'll settle for absolutely anything right now. Please just squeeze my hand—but there's no movement. It's difficult to know what to say and I feel awkward speaking to you whilst you're still, especially when the nurses are around. You look so peaceful compared to how I feel.

I've lied and told you that me and the girls are just fine, that everything is OK and they are safely at home with your parents. We're not fine though, are we? The girls are sat with a staff nurse in my side room downstairs, suffering from shock and desperate to see their daddy. We're so far removed from fine, we're possibly scarred for life. I'm guessing we'll be in therapy for the next six months at least, then Christ only knows.

The air in this place is sterile, claustrophobic. It's

a struggle to breathe. My only comfort is this damn wheelchair but it makes it difficult for me to get close enough to you.

The nurses check and probe you every fifteen minutes, flashing a torchlight into your eyes. We are all praying for a response. They scribble notes, mark your charts and they share the same look of concern. They've combed your hair straight, scraped it back and off your face, not knowing that you prefer your blond curls natural, clean, and wavy as they fall when you're first out of bed. Now it looks darker, oily, more severe. I've always envied your olive skin, how you tan after one day in the sun, unlike me. But now it's grey, wax-like and drained of all form of life. I'm desperate for those kind brown eyes to open, to acknowledge me, to want me.

Just sit up, babe, hold me in your arms and we can delete the past twenty-four hours, pretend it didn't happen and we can all go back home. That's not going to happen though, is it? This could go on for months. I need to buy you some decent pyjamas too because that hospital gown swamps you, even after all those relentless gym sessions. You look frail, weak and delicate. Your limbs are motionless. It's impossible for me to get too close, impossible to get past these tubes, drips and drains that are busy keeping you alive. The incessant beep of machinery monitors every beat of your heart and the hissing oxygen fills your lungs.

You fell hard to the floor, babe. Ten years of married bliss flashed before me, and I thought you were gone. How do I tell you that I'm too petrified to sleep? That when my mind drifts, his soulless eyes burn straight through me. I can't tell you that I'm desperate to scrub my skin raw to remove the stench of his body odour. That I want to bleach my mouth and remove the smell of his booze and his stale cigarettes, from when he forced himself upon me.

I can't tell you any of that yet though, can I? In fact, will I ever be able to tell you? Will you recover from any of this?

2

If I say anything right now, could it make you worse, stress you out, drive you deeper into your unconscious sleep? You'd only blame yourself, of course, that goes without saying. That you hadn't saved me, that you were the one determined we should leave that door open, the door that led out to the woods. How you insisted, despite knowing I was afraid of the dark. I suppose he saw the new 4x4 parked outside, thought we were rich, easy pickings.

So for now I've buried my thoughts and my fears and continue to tell you just how much you are loved, how much we want you, and how much we need you to open your eyes, to come back to us. This is all I can do right now.

My left foot is in absolute agony, stabbing and burning intermittently, like red hot irons melting through my skin. My head is muzzy with painkillers and a cocktail of medication from the staff, their attempt to keep me calm.

Meanwhile, the rounds of gunshots keep firing and last night's terror continues looping, testing me over and over. Even in my moments of clarity, the gunfire is real, still there, playing cruel games with my head. Driving me crazy.

Twenty-four hours ago, we were at that idyllic log cabin, deep in the forest. The adorable bank holiday retreat, perfect weather, perfect place. Just me, you and the twins— there to relax and have some fun, there to get *you* to slow down and spend quality time with us, something that has been lacking recently.

Now all that's left is a lifelong memory, just for some jewellery and cash. It doesn't make sense. Yesterday seems like a lifetime ago. Will we ever get over this? Will we ever get back to the way we were?

I'm losing it. I scream and do all the things they told me not to do. "Come on, for God's sake, Will, I need you to wake up!" I'm terrified he's coming back, back to get us, me you and the girls, to finish off the job. "Just open your eyes, please babe. I need you, we need you. Just open your bloody eyes! Will, please." I grab your pyjama shoulders, drag you towards my chest, but your lifeless head sinks back into the pillow. That's when I lose it, when I practically attack you. "Wake up! Wake up, Will, please!"

Your monitors go haywire, the shrill alarms pierce through me, and a team of nurses push past me, injecting you, injecting me.

2

When I wake up I am back downstairs in my side room, confused and groggy—I guess from the drugs. How long have I been out? I really don't know, nor do I have the faintest idea what time of day, or day of the week it is for that matter. My only small comfort is my girls, their tiny bodies asleep by my side. I buzz for a nurse, anxious to know how you are. Just what the hell happened upstairs? What was I thinking?

"How's my husband?" I whisper, careful not to wake the twins.

I remember screaming and shaking you, insisting you wake up, but now I'm so embarrassed and feeling like some crazy woman for my outburst. I think the staff nurse can't quite make me out either. Is she deeply sorry for me or does she think I'm a total psycho? It's hard to tell.

"I'll get the doctor to speak to you, honey. He's here on the ward at the moment. He shouldn't be long."

He arrives in his pressed white coat; he's probably the same age as me if not a little bit younger, maybe late twenties. His eyes are kind and sympathetic. He's not dissimilar to you—tall, lean and athletic—makes me want you all the more.

"Karen, sorry, we had no choice but to sedate you. You were hysterical. You tried to wake your husband and it set his monitors off. Apologies, but our hands were tied. You sent his heart racing to a dangerous level. On the one hand, it's good that he heard you, but we just don't need him unnecessarily stressed at the moment. He needs calm, rest, time to regain consciousness."

"I'm so sorry, that's not like me. Oh God, have I made him worse?"

"No, there's no change, there's no further damage. You can go back up there but may I suggest you get some rest here before you do. Don't rush it. What you did is perfectly understandable; I probably would have done the same thing in your circumstances. You've had a nasty attack. You'll be traumatised for some time. Your recovery could take months, not weeks. We have excellent counsellors here so make good use of them; your whole family would benefit from some type of therapy."

The door closes and again I feel isolated. Even though the girls are by my side, I'm so lost without you. The problem is that leaving me on my own just adds to my thinking time, time to reflect on the last couple of days. I try to concentrate on the twelve hours leading up to Saturday night, before it all went horribly wrong, positive thoughts. It was supposed to have been an idyllic weekend away. Only twenty minutes from home, no airplane to catch, no May bank holiday chaos. The idea was you could de-stress and chill. You'd been so uptight lately, constantly texting or making late night phone calls. Recently your mobile was attached to you twenty-four seven. I guessed it was deals being made, hoped and prayed it wasn't another woman.

Although, if I'm honest, that's exactly what I imagined was going on. You were showing all the classic signs of a man having a fling: trips to the gym four times a week, taking your phone everywhere, even to the bathroom, and you looked permanently stressed. Your moods blew hot and cold, especially when we reached the log cabin. You were particularly on edge, like you just didn't want to be there—a side to you I hadn't seen before. I wanted to make things special for us. I wanted it all to be perfect, like the old days. The weather forecast was set for a heatwave, unusual for that time of year at 79 degrees plus. It was going to be a scorcher.

The idyllic cabin with its heady pine wood aroma was set deep in the secluded Cheshire forest, a perfect place to drink fine wines, eat *al fresco* and just chill out. Our twins had been beyond excited and desperate to play in the hot tub. We were all on a high; even you eventually were showing signs of coming back down to earth. An exciting few days lay ahead.

The interior of the cabin had been designed tastefully to make you feel you'd been whisked away from civilisation, maybe somewhere deep in the Rocky mountains of Canada, or up in some five star alpine ski lodge.

The central focus of the main living space was a ready-to-light wood burner with extra logs stacked neatly either side. The wood gave off a rich oaky aroma which filled every room in the cabin. Two highly polished brown leather Chesterfields sat proudly either side of the fireplace and a sumptuous black and white rug was perfectly placed on the floor. Three sets of wooden skis hung on the walls and a child's antique sledge was placed against the woodwork underneath a large set of reindeer horns. Between the lounge and the kitchen were wooden patio doors that led out to a neat little garden surrounded by dense fir trees. The hot tub was sunken into the ground at the far end of the garden, all ready and waiting for us to indulge.

The owner had left us a welcome pack consisting of a bottle of Chateau Neuf du Pape, some fine French cheeses, two fresh French sticks and a large box of milk chocolates.

"This cabin wouldn't be out of place in the middle of a Swiss village. Well done, babe!" You placed your arm around my waist and pulled me close.

We were so chuffed. Our bedroom had a door that led out to a cute little balcony facing the forest, with a patio table and two chairs, the perfect place for my morning coffee.

That's where it all went wrong though, wasn't it—mistake number one. You complained you were too hot that night; the bloody air con wasn't working so you decided to leave the patio door open. You knew I wasn't happy. I didn't have a problem with my body temperature, I was permanently at least three degrees cooler than you. You knew I had a fear of the dark and often ridiculed me, but you insisted. Leaving that door open was something we would never have done at home. We were asking for trouble.

That's exactly where he came in. When he woke me up at about two in the morning, I was convinced I was dreaming and would snap out of my nightmare, but instead our ordeal had only just begun. A little something that would haunt us forever. At first, I thought it was you. I was convinced you'd got up to go to the loo, too many beers, but you were oblivious. I could feel the heat from your body next to me. You were sound asleep and snoring without a care in the world. I was petrified. Someone or something was there, in our bedroom, rifling through *our* things. I couldn't see but I knew it was human. The air was thick and warm, enhancing his stench of stale cigarettes, booze and body odour, making my stomach churn. I slowly inhaled and said nothing, holding onto my breath and pretending to be fast asleep.

The room was stifling, airless, and the sweat trickled down my back against my dry, hot skin. With my eyes closed, I prayed maybe he would go away. My heart was lodged firmly in my throat, blood pulsing in my neck as I tried desperately to control my breathing. I had to keep it together. If he found nothing, maybe he'd just leave us alone, maybe he'd just go away. I had to stay quiet and calm for all our sakes. If I disturbed him, who knew what he'd do?

You were snoring so loudly. How could you possibly sleep when some mad man was right there, in *our* bedroom, rummaging through *our* things? *God help us, please God help us*, I chanted over and over in my head. *Stay calm, breathe, Karen, breathe*. For God's sake, Will, I needed you to wake up, to save us. It seemed as if he had been there for an eternity, not minutes.

Finally, you woke up with a jolt when he stumbled in the dark and knocked the suitcase crashing against the wall. He rammed his gun firmly on your forehead. The dark woollen ski mask concealed his face, revealing two soulless eyes, teeth clenched tight together as he spat out the words.

"If you make one fucking sound, I will kill your wife and the brats."

Christ, how did he know we had kids? Had he been in their room first? Had he been watching us? It was over—our life, our girls, us. What next? I sat bolt upright, grabbing the covers tight against my skin. Shaking and sweating, my face burning like a furnace. He lunged at my arm, dragged me naked into the kitchen. Where were you though, Will? I expected you to follow me, to save me, but not a sound from you. What was going on? Where were you? Why didn't you come?

I snatched your brown jacket, held it close, desperately trying to cover every inch of flesh. Even with his ski mask on, I could feel his eyes crawling all over me.

"Very nice. Shall I just get my money's worth from you,

Karen?" he laughed. "Where's your money, bitch, your jewellery, your cards? Where the fuck is it?"

My mind blanked; I couldn't think straight, let alone speak. We only had £50 as we'd struggled to find a cash point on the way.

For God's sake, Will, I thought you would be straight in there to save me, but just what the hell were you doing? What was going on? I tore at my jewellery, desperately tugging at my rings. Some of my bangles and bracelets were already on the table from earlier. I knew I should have left them at home, but you insisted though, didn't you, that I wore all the expensive stuff. "T…Take," was all I managed to say.

"I want you and I want your money," he growled. "You're with me. Get a coat, get your cards and get your car keys. We are going for a little ride. It's payback time."

Payback for what? He rammed my jewellery into his left-hand pocket and indicated with his gun towards the front door.

"Oh my God, just take the car and my cards, please. I'll give you the PIN numbers. I promise we won't tell the police."

"Oh yeah, right," he laughed sarcastically. He pushed the gun hard against my throat, tilting my head to one side. "Move, you fuckin' stupid bitch!" he screamed as he staggered nearer, sending the chair crashing onto the ceramic floor.   Where were you, Will? I threw on your brown jacket and the shorts you had left on the back of the chair, my hands visibly quaking, struggling to fasten up, struggling to keep covered. I shook my bag upside down on the kitchen table, anxious to get the bank cards, the car keys and my phone. Why my mobile, I've no clue, habit perhaps.

Down the corridor, the bedroom door crashed hard against the wall.

"You fuckin' bastard! Leave her," you growled, charging

at him, sending the table and the remaining contents of my bag flying across the room. At last you were there to save us. Shafts of moonlight through the windows allowed me to catch glimpses of the horror unfolding in front of me. I'd never heard you even raise your voice before, let alone fight. Brief moments seemed eternal—the grunts, the shouts, the scuffling on the floor. Then there was an ominous silence. I could see you and you appeared to have the upper hand as you straddled him and attempted to straighten up.

"Thank God," I whispered.

Nothing else would come from my mouth, the words trapped within me. It was over. Finally, you had saved us. Until one click—a strobe of light filled the room, a gunshot! You grabbed your leg, falling backwards, your face showing the shock, the terror, the disbelief. You dropped hard to the floor, screaming, "You bastard!"

I fell to my knees, my hand pushed tight, covering my mouth.

Shot number two—click, then bang. Your body jolted, clearly hit again, but where this time? It was impossible to see, the light only lasted split seconds.

"Ahhh, fuck..." I heard you slur.

Shot number three—click, and bang. Nothing, no sound, no movement from you. A high-pitched ringing filled my head. I could only manage to distinguish muffled sounds. I prayed for you to stand, to grab me, to hold me close. But it wasn't you, was it? It was him. You didn't stand a chance.

He steadied himself, still brandishing his gun, and staggered towards me, grabbed me to my feet, leaving you lying on the floor, motionless in a rapidly spreading pool of black blood.

"Oh, my God! N... n... no, Will, no!" My own words stuck in my throat.

I thought you were dead. I thought you were gone—

forever.

The girls were stirring in their room, obviously panicked. They had to stay there, they had to stay safe. Moments later their petrified faces peered around their door as they clung tight to each other, my babies.

"M... M... Mum, D... D... ad."

"Stay, shhh." I placed my finger over my mouth. "Don't move. I'm OK!"

Christ, would he take them too, instead of me. They needed to stay there. If they left their room, would he take us all?

I'm shaking uncontrollably. The girls are beside me with not a care, sound asleep. I have to get my head together. The antiseptic air in this room is stifling. I buzz for the nurse again. "Please give me something to calm me, anything, I don't care. Anything to wipe this from my head," I plead. Will, I need you so badly now, to talk to, to hold me, to share this horror, to tell me everything will be alright.

You are asleep, though, aren't you! One floor above, still out of it, still motionless, still at peace. But what if you never wake up, never come back to us? What if your brain is damaged, perhaps with a total personality change? I have to stop torturing myself. I need to see you.

When she returns with the tablets I ask, "When can I see my husband?"

"I'll get you a wheelchair, honey, and a porter. I'll stay with your girls whilst you go up to intensive care."

"Thank you so much," I whisper. I need to get a grip for the sake of the twins.

A porter arrives with a wheelchair. He chats all the way to ITU, something about his recent holiday to Spain. I'm not paying attention, too busy thinking about you. The pain in my foot had eased off slightly, thanks to the pills.

When we reach Intensive Care it is a hive of activity; three new patients have been admitted since yesterday.

Things haven't changed with you, though. You are still unconscious, still lifeless. Your heart monitor beeps away nicely and the saline drip slowly feeds your veins. To the left of the bed is a drain filled with your dark crimson blood, blood from your leg. I try not to look. I was never good with that sort of thing, was I! You look so helpless. So many machines surround you, but at least you are at peace with the same calm expression on your face, a total contrast to me being so stressed out, a total wreck. The room is warm, dry and stuffy. Even though there is still a heatwave going on outside, the central heating is still on full power. The relentless tone of the beeps is starting to irritate me. Streams of tears wash my face and I don't know what to do. I just feel helpless, and so I speak gently to you.

"Love you, hun. You're going to be OK; me and the girls will help you get better. We all love you so, so much. Please wake up, sweetheart, I love you. Please can you just open your eyes."

I stroke your hand, hoping you will wake, so we can leave here and it would all go away. Maybe it was some kind of a sick joke. We've been through so much. The ski mask keeps haunting me. All I can see is his eyes, etched in my head probably forever. My gut feeling is that he is on his way back to finish us off.

3

Sunday May Bank Holiday 2.45pm

We all manage to get a few hours' sleep. The staff nurse, once again, is sitting with the twins and I'm back upstairs with you, but there's still no change.

"Hi sweetheart, let me give you a kiss," I say as if you're wide awake and *compos menti*s. I find it easier to speak to you now. I guess I'm slowly getting used to this. Even though there's no response, I just ramble on about anything to you regardless; no doubt you will moan at me when—or if—you finally wake up. I have no clue what tablets they've given me, but it's definitely taken the edge off, a bit like my head after a few glasses of prosecco. It's a comforting haze.

Running out of things to say, I decide to start talking to you about Mum.

When forced into a situation like this, it makes you sit up, evaluate your life, puts things into perspective. Looking back, Mum's problems were enormous to me at the time. My tireless visits to her apartment, the not quite knowing

15

what I was going to find next, but even they seem so trivial compared to the mess we have to deal with right now.

Last November—just seven months back, seems like years ago—we were in bed, remember? It was the night the storm gave our garden a good battering. The night our magnolia was split in two by the fern tree falling smack bang in the middle of it. Our girls were too frightened to sleep in their own rooms, thanks to the howling wind, so we let them bring their quilts into our room and they slept on the *chaise longue*. The phone rang, 2am. I snatched at the handset, not wanting to wake you all. I knew too well who it was. Maybe the storm had scared her too.

"Karen, Karen! Is that you? Where the bloody hell are you? What time do you call this? Oh, you're in trouble when you get in, your dad will go mad. Get yourself home right now! Right now, young lady!"

"Mum, calm down, listen to me. I'm not at home any more, remember. I'm married, aren't I? I'm married to Will. It's two o'clock in the morning. You have grandchildren. The twins, Ellie and Jesse, you do remember? It's late. Calm yourself down. Get some sleep. Don't worry about me. Go back to bed. I'll be round in the morning." There had been a long pause followed by her sobbing down the phone as I tried to hold back my tears. "Let's get some sleep and I'll see you first thing. I promise, OK? You've just had a bad dream. Goodnight, I love you. Now go back to bed."

You pulled me close, Will.

"How can she forget that her own husband is dead? Dad's been gone three years!"

"She's going to need help from the professionals soon, hun, you realise that, don't you?" You were insistent.

"Not now, Will. Mum's not going in a home. I'm not talking about this now."

"I hate to say it, but in the long run it will be the best place for her, and the best thing for you. Look at you;

16

you're knackered going over there all the time. You can't keep this up. You're making yourself ill."

"Not now. Goodnight." My face soaked in tears, I tossed and turned until, eventually about fiveish, I think I fell asleep.

The next morning was frosty and glorious, do you remember? Not a cloud in the sky. We'd planned to get the last of the garden bulbs in that weekend, but thanks to the storm you had a couple of trees to deal with first. Outside was still, except for the occasional rumble of traffic from the A50. You let me sleep whilst you sorted breakfast. The girls were full of beans, listening to Britney, and dancing like crazy around the kitchen. They looked like mini versions of you, only their curly blonde hair fell way below their shoulders. Unmistakably yours, with those ever-smiling brown eyes. Ellie is going to be the entertainer in the family, with her long blonde locks framing her imp-like cheeky smile. Almost as tall as me, even at ten, she is the tomboy of the two, the protective one. Jesse is more like you, I guess, with her slightly more serious side: thoughtful, quieter, more of a girlie than Ellie. Even though she is only a few minutes younger, she is definitely our baby of the family. They were both dancing to "Oops I did it again". We didn't need telly anymore, did we? Not with those two around.

"OK ladies, who's for bacon and eggs?"

"Me."

"Me too, Dad."

"Set the table for us then."

I was exhausted, but tried to put on a brave face for the sake of the girls. My eyes were puffy, swollen and tight.

It was freezing outside, a few branches were down as well as the trees, the remaining leaves danced around and swirled like mini tornados, the birdsong absent, so I closed the window then poured us tea into two huge mugs and faced you. You talked about a home in the village, how ideal it was that it was nearer, with an excellent reputation. How we should go and view it. I shouted, remember?

"Stop it, Will, I can't talk about this now. Give me a break. I'm going to see Mum in half an hour, just to make sure she's alright."

"Why, Mum? What happened? Is Nanny OK?"

"Yeah, she's fine, sweetheart."

"Can we come with you?" Bless Jesse.

"Not today, maybe in a few days' time."

I left the house late morning about elevenish and drove on autopilot to Mum's apartment. My head was all over the place. I was completely knackered from the early morning call, having had just three hours' sleep, worrying, tossing and turning and remembering your words: "It's time she went into a home, hun." Turning right into the car park, I sat motionless, trying to compose myself. What was I going to find this time? I'd sat in my car so many times knowing she would have forgotten my visit. Later she'd be on the phone. "I'm OK, love, there's plenty of shopping in the fridge, my house is tidy. You know I'm fine. When are you coming over next?" Only it was me who did the shopping, the cleaning, the washing, the ironing. Mum's short-term memory was fading rapidly. You were right, she did need professional medical care. We had to get her a diagnosis—although half of me didn't want to know the truth. I dreaded an Alzheimer's diagnosis. It ran in her family. Aunty Jane ended up in a care home for twelve long years that broke Mum's heart. The problem was that Mum hadn't been near a doctor in twenty-odd years. Getting her to see someone wasn't going to be an easy task. She is such a proud and stubborn woman.

"Mum?" I knocked on the door, but there was no reply. "Mum, answer the door please, it's Karen!" There were confused mumbles from inside but she wouldn't, or worse, couldn't get it open. I'd bought your bloody car keys instead of mine, and her front door keys were on my set at home. I could have kicked myself. What an idiot! "Just let me in!" It was a freezing day, minus three. I'd left my gloves in the car so I blew into my hands to try to keep them warm. Now I was starting to lose it. "Mum, open the door. It's cold out here!" But still the mumbling, whimpering. "Open up!"

I vaguely remembered a spare key somewhere in the old shed. Dad would often forget to take his keys, so they left a spare just in case. I darted across the courtyard. The door handle was frozen and rusty, so it was tough to move and my hands were starting to go numb. But after a few sharp jolts I managed to force it open. The stale stench of dry treated wood hit me as I scrambled through the graveyard of belongings scattered around inside: Dad's old lawn mower, his work tools, broomsticks. His shrine completely untouched and now coated in thick, dusty cobwebs. Above was a colony of spiders, ready to pounce at any given moment. The shed hadn't been used for years, four in fact. Dad had been ill with heart problems for a good year before he passed. How could she forget her own husband dying? "Got it," I'd muttered under my breath. Underneath a watering can doused in thick, sticky cobwebs was the much-needed door key. I grabbed it and ran.

With shaking hands, I turned the key and tried to squeeze through the door, conscious not to hurt or move her. She was lying on her back on the cold ceramic floor, her leg twisted in a seemingly impossible position. It was obviously broken.

"I was cooking tea for your dad," she babbled.

I spoke gently to her. "It's OK, Mum, I'm here now. Don't worry."

We were lying on the cold hallway floor as we waited for the sound of sirens. I'd wrapped her with a thick blanket, held her tight, and tried to warm her tiny hands. She must have been lying on that floor for hours. I felt awful. I should have driven over early this morning when she called. "What are we going to do with you?" I whispered.

I'd had to hold my breath when I went in. The two-bed apartment was filthy; the air reeked of stale dried urine. Used pads and underwear were abandoned on the floor throughout the flat. She looked like she'd slept in the bathroom—that was a new one—with the soiled blanket and pillow as evidence, crumpled in a corner.

It wasn't so long ago Mum had been such a proud woman: smart, tidy, immaculate, not a thing out of place. In earlier days, the apartment had been spotless: ornaments tastefully chosen and dotted around each room. It was neat, compact, with its small square of garden, their perfect haven.

Since Dad died, Mum's condition had spiralled. Her depression set in fast and her flat refusal to visit the hairdressers resulted in a dishevelled appearance: her hair had become grey, wild and long. She clearly didn't care anymore. What remained of a once youthful physique was now a frail, wizened old lady. She lived off ham sandwiches, bananas and copious amounts of tea which added to her bladder problem. Twelve pictures decorated her wall, various images of the three of us together in happier times; she used to be so glamorous. In the space of three short years she had aged at least ten.

The ambulance men arrived and went through their routine questions with us.

"She has severe memory problems," I explained through broken sobs.

"Don't take me away, there's nothing wrong with me. Karen can look after me," she pleaded. "I can go to my daughter's house. Don't let them take me, Karen!"

"Mum, you need to see a doctor."

"Mary, we are taking you to hospital, you've broken your leg badly."

"I'm coming with you," I tried to reassure her. "I'm not going to leave you, am I? Let's see the doctor together.

They can fix your leg. OK?" I sat beside her, holding her tight.

One good thing was once we were at the hospital she would finally be in the system. You were right, Will. Mum couldn't cope. I called you from my mobile.

"Hi hun, I'm at the hospital with Mum, she's broken her leg. I'm going to stay here for a while. I'll call you later."

"Ah dol, I'm so sorry. She's in the right place now, you know that."

"Thanks. Must go. I need to give them her details. Call you later."

"Love you. Give her a kiss from me and the girls."

"Will do. Thanks, hun." You were so sweet to me, always so caring and supportive—well, until recently.

I'd never known Mum to be poorly in my lifetime, not even a cold, let alone see a doctor. I was always the sickly one of the family, I was the one with bronchitis every five weeks. She'd be the one taking me on endless trips to the doctor's. So now social services would be on the case. If I am honest, it had to happen, you were right, but it broke my heart. She was in their hands. More importantly for me, she would be surrounded by people all day long, not in solitary confinement as she had been for the past three years, except for visits from me. I must admit I was relieved.

When she returned from theatre she was groggy, babbling confused words and very agitated. She kept trying to get out of bed, even with her leg secured in a full-length plaster which was enormous against her tiny frame. She'd also had a good tug at the drip taped firmly to the back of her hand. I voiced my concerns to the senior nurse. They had to sedate her to keep her safe.

"I think my mum has Alzheimer's or dementia. She's never been assessed. Her memory has been going downhill rapidly since my dad died three years ago."

"Let's get her leg sorted first then we can deal with

21

her other problems. I'll set up an appointment with the psychiatrist. Once we have a diagnosis we can get social services to have a chat with you and get a plan into action between us all."

It was all a bit overwhelming. Thank God she had broken her leg. As cruel as it sounds, this had been a long time coming and at least it felt like something was finally being done. I decided to stay for another three hours. I needed to be there for her when she woke up. She was only lucid for moments and she was clearly confused. It broke my heart. The staff gave her some strong painkillers, more sedation and she remained sound asleep.

What a day that was both mentally and physically. Eventually I was back in the comfort of my car. I couldn't wait to get home to chill out with you and the girls, put my feet up and maybe watch something uplifting on the telly. I switched on the car radio but every tune reminded me of them, of my parents. Memories of the old days, hot summer holidays in Porthleven, Cornwall, staying in some tatty old campsite with Mum and Dad. Dad and I outside the campervan playing bat and ball. He was always being daft in some way or another. Mum singing along to Diana Ross on the radio with a hairbrush for a microphone. It was all too much. I couldn't wait to see you and the girls. I was completely exhausted and needed one of your hugs.

Bless you, you made me want to cry, there in the kitchen with your *Ready Steady Cook* apron on, singing along to David Bowie's "Heroes". You'd prepared my favourite dish, which was warming in the oven. *Spag Bol Will*, as you call it. A huge glass of dry white wine was there, all ready and waiting.

"Thanks, hun. It's been a really crap day. Mum looked so frail and helpless lying there in the bed. Still, she's much more peaceful than she was this morning... she was so cold, so confused. She must have been on the floor for ages."

You held me tight. I was inconsolable, but you wiped

my tears with the tea towel and ushered me towards the kitchen table.

"Eat, build your strength up, you're going to need it. She needs you healthy, we all do." Bless you, always so kind and caring.

Ellie and Jesse were clingy that night too, seeing me so distraught and well aware that something was wrong with Nanny.

"Thanks for my lovely hugs, kids; thanks, Will, for everything."

"Come on, have another glass of wine, then why don't you go to bed, babe? Get some rest, put the telly on upstairs."

"Can we watch it in bed with you, Mum?"

"Great idea! Come on then, ladies, let's all snuggle upstairs for half an hour. How does that sound?"

"Yeah!"

Without another word, the sound of two pairs of stockinged feet could be heard bounding up the stairs, gone before I'd finished my wine. When I joined them, the cushions were all reorganised with a space just big enough for me to squeeze in, between them and a selection of their teddies. "So we're watching the X Factor then, are we?" That was the first time I'd laughed that day.

Sorry for rambling, hun. I know I was going off at a tangent there talking about Mum, when the real problem is right here right now, you and the uncertainty of whether or not you will wake up from your sleep. Even though they've told me it's a matter of time, to let the brain swelling to go down, there is a high likelihood that you will wake up. Problem is what will you be like when you do come round? Will you still be the same? People have been known to have a total character change. Will you make a full recovery? Will you be able to walk? Why am I doing this? I'm just torturing myself. I've had years of dealing

23

with Mum and her confusion. Are you going to be the same? Is your personality going to change too?

It was becoming increasingly obvious to all the nursing staff that Mum was indeed a very confused lady. Sadly, the broken leg had sealed her future. The staff approached me to talk about getting a professional diagnosis. All the wheels were in motion now, you were right. I just didn't want to admit it. So, the day was booked for her to see a psychiatrist and hopefully get some answers. I stayed with Mum and sat at the back of the room whilst the doctor gave her some simple memory tests.

"Mary, I'm going to tell you an address. I want you to try to remember it then later I will ask you for the address again. Is that OK?"

"Of course. I don't know what all the fuss is all about; there's nothing wrong with me."

Bless her. I could feel a lump in my throat. Mum is a little sweetie; she looked so much older sitting in that consulting room.

"Fifty-four Smith Street, Lancashire. Have you got that?"

"Yes, that's a nice easy one to remember."

She was so adorable, so polite, she broke my heart. She answered every single question perfectly. The psychiatrist continued through his standard list. She was completely brilliant and an outsider wouldn't have known anything was wrong with her. That was, until he asked her the date.

"What day is it today then, Mary?"

"Ooh every day's a Sunday," she laughed, her little joke. "Thursday, I think."

A good guess, I thought. She got that one right.

"OK and what month?"

"Ooh February, March, I don't keep track these days, since I've retired," she laughed again, not realising the importance of each question.

"OK, Mary, which year?"

"1990…"

What? I couldn't believe it! She was thirty years out. She had been perfect all the way through the test and had royally blown it right at the very end. In a way, it was a relief for me because it certainly highlighted her problem. Mum was locked into her memory of 1990. In her defence, it was a pretty amazing year. Dad was doing great work-wise; he'd gone self-employed that year, was working every hour God sent and was paid handsomely. We went on a three-week holiday to the Algarve in Portugal, not a cloud in the sky, hired the most enormous villa and invited good friends out there to join us at various times. Probably the best holiday we'd ever had; a total contrast to those campsites in Cornwall.

"So, Mary, can you tell me the address I gave you to remember at the beginning of our conversation?"

"Oh… Oh I can't remember that, I can't remember what happened this morning. My memory is shocking these days, you know," she laughed.

Bless her. And there it was. It amazed me at how perfectly she'd answered each question; it appeared as if there was, in fact, absolutely nothing wrong with her memory, right up until those last fateful sentences.

After the test, we ventured downstairs to the hospital café for some much-needed quality time.

"So, where's Dad?"

"What?" She'd stopped me in my tracks. I couldn't believe my bloody ears; she'd done it again. She had been word perfect with the doctor, until the 1990 blip, and then to say something so outrageous. Dad had been gone for three years, for God's sake.

In the early days, my grief had been so extreme I couldn't leave the house the first month following his death; just collecting the girls from school took all my effort. Breaking down in floods of tears at the drop of a hat was the norm. A simple old Nat King Cole song on the radio would set me off. So many men resembled him from behind. I had been known to follow a few old chaps just because they had a Bristol accent like him. Then to see how it affected Mum. I guess a large part of her had died too, along with her husband. It made me so angry to hear her say those words. How the bloody hell could she forget something so monumental.

I was livid, so I ignored the question. Why answer it? It would only reduce her to tears, so I just changed the subject. That aside, we had a lovely hour or so together. I took her for lunch. It wasn't your typical hospital café, it was a bit of a haven. I think some of the décor must have been funded by charity: brown leather chairs, black velour cushions, black and white photos tastefully mounted in black frames, more like the interior of a Café Nero than the usual NHS canteen. I ordered us both a hot chocolate and a cream tea, a favourite of ours from the past. It was always our little treat on the way to weekends in Devon and Cornwall. Dad used to cover his face with clotted cream, just to make us laugh. He hated cakes but he was always doing crazy things. Loving scones and jam was something that bonded Mum and I and the fond recollections gave me a warm glow. I was snapped out of my memories by a saucer being dropped behind the till. Time had whizzed by and we had to get back up to the ward. Her leg was causing her problems and she looked like she could do with some pain relief. The fall had aged her at least another ten years. Seeing her shuffling with her tiny frame was so depressing. Mum was fading away before my very eyes.

Is the same happening to you, Will? I squeeze your hand then settle back, watching you in silence as the monitors continue to beep.

4

Sunday May Bank Holiday 3.30pm

The porter drops me back in my room. I have to get some composure for the sake of our girls, bless them. I've only been with you for about half an hour but they seem so desperate to see me. As kind as the staff nurse is, they both leap off my bed and grab me from either side of the wheelchair.

"Karen, do you have any numbers we can ring for parents, friends?"

"If you could ring my husband's parents. My father died three years ago and my mother has memory problems, so there's no need to upset her." Oh Jesus, how on earth will I explain this to her? Is there any point? She'd only be distressed and then forget the entire conversation. The one time when I really need her, the one time I could do with some comfort from my mother. It is best not to say anything, keep it to myself. It might make her worse, confuse her even more, accelerate her condition.

Your parents are the only numbers I can think of, as

there is no point phoning your brother, he hasn't spoken to you for over ten years. He still blames you for Jeanie.

Within forty minutes they've arrived from Wales, they must have driven like crazy. They idolise you, me and the girls. Thank God we have one set of parents for support. Your mum looks like she's had a good cry on the way. We hold each other tight as though trying to squeeze the demons away.

"We can take the girls back to yours, if you like, let you get some rest."

I try to explain the events of the previous night but am so choked; the words won't come out.

"Listen, the main thing is you're all alive."

I don't know what I would do without them. They know you're unconscious, but still they stay with us for half an hour before going to see you in intensive care, just in case you wake up. Your mum said she broke down, seeing you lying there motionless, with the cradle under your covers protecting your wound.

Ellie, Jesse and I lie side by side, falling in and out of sleep in sheer exhaustion. A couple of hours pass; I wake up with your parents back in my room cuddling the twins, each has one of the girls on their knee. My eyes scan the room. We all have red puffy eyes set in ashen faces. The nurse from the early shift brings us yet more tea. It is a relief to hear a cheery voice.

"Hey girls, why don't you come with me and I'll take you both out into our lovely Zen garden, get a bit of fresh air? Let these grown-ups talk for a while. Is that OK with you, Mum?"

"Is that OK, Mummy?" They half smile. I can tell they don't want to go. The trauma of the past twenty-four hours has taken its toll. They don't deserve this—none of us do. We should have been at the log cabin, playing in the hot tub and soaking up the fresh air, not stuck in a stuffy side ward, grief stricken.

"Sure kids, that's a great idea."

They leave us reluctantly; I can tell they are not the slightest bit interested in seeing some Zen garden. They have become understandably clingy, almost like toddlers again. I don't want them or anybody else to leave me; I want to keep everyone close and safe but I have to talk to your parents.

As soon as they leave, your mum collapses in grief. I've never seen her like this before.

"How, Karen? What on earth? Is our Will ever going to wake up? And if he does, how are you all going to manage? Will he be the same? What if he's brain damaged? How's our Will going to cope … work … function?" Your dad places his arm around her shoulders, but he too needs comforting. She's babbling, making little sense, wringing her hands. He's choked too and keeps clearing his throat, neither of them knowing what to say.

I don't make much sense either, if I'm honest. I just keep reliving and torturing myself with the 'if only's: If only we hadn't left the back door open; if only I hadn't bid for that bloody log cabin. My head is all over the place, trying to predict what's going to happen next, what is going to happen to us all. My head is playing the tape, relentless images: the nightmare, the soulless eyes. Who was that bastard? Why did he attack us? What could have happened? Would he have killed us? It is draining me, and my brain just won't switch off. I need to compose myself for the sake of my girls, for you. I need to be strong for all our sakes.

"We were so stupid. We left the outside bedroom door open, it led out to the forest." I feel I have to explain at least something to your parents. "Will was too hot, the air-con was faulty. We'd never normally do that, but he insisted. That's how this madman got into our room. I could just about see him, but Will was fast asleep. I was petrified so

I tried to stay still, hoped he might go, find nothing and leave, but he didn't. Instead, he knocked something over and Will woke up. He had a gun to Will's head. I thought Will was dead. I thought he was dead." I'm off again. "What are we going to do?" I explain how he forced me drive to the cashpoint with a gun to my throat and then shot me in the foot. As I relive the events it makes me even more distraught. "How's Will? Was he awake when you went up there?"

"No, he's still not come round yet, and he's still on morphine for the time being. I have spoken to one of the doctors and he's happy it all went well. Now we just have to wait for him to come round. Hope that his brain isn't ... damaged. The surgeon wants to talk to me later as well." Your father coughs to try to clear his throat. "They hope his wound doesn't become infected and that he heals quickly." His voice quivers as he tries desperately to compose himself. "It's going to take time, love, a very long time."

Ellie and Jesse are back in the room after twenty minutes, still looking grey but a hint of peach touches their cheeks after being in the fresh air. Your parents offer to take them home, let them sleep, and bring them back later after some tea, but the girls don't want to leave me.

"We're not going, Mum." They both squeeze me tight. "Please don't make us go."

I hug them, stroke their hair then hold them at arm's length, looking into their eyes, so like yours.

"Listen to me, you saved your daddy's life." I embrace them again, this time as if it is my last. They both look so frail, so thin, their eyes now red raw with tears. We've got through our first day of trauma, but this is just the beginning and we need to be strong. "Why don't you go home for a while. Granny and Grandpops are right. Go sleep, eat something nice for tea and I'll see you all later tonight, I promise."

"OK, Mum, love you." They both nod, trying to be brave, their faces showing the extent of their terror.

"I love you both too. I'm so proud of you ... so, so much."

The door closes and it breaks my heart to see them go, especially with this maniac on the loose.

5

Sunday May Bank Holiday 5.00pm

Without you, I'm lost. What do I do with myself? I don't want to be isolated. The girls are back at home with your parents. Would I be better off on a large ward, with people around me, someone to talk to and take my mind off things? From the minute I wake, all I do is think—about you, about our girls and about that haunting balaclava. When I sleep, the whole horror kicks in again, torturing me relentlessly. I am exhausted: tablets to help me sleep, tablets to calm me down, tablets for the pain. To be honest, I'm struggling.

I can't stand my own company any longer, so I go back up to ITU to sit with you. The staff have been warned this time though. They have moved you nearer to the nurse's station to keep an eye on me, keep an eye on the crazy wife. I am convinced they are checking on you more frequently than before. Maybe they think I'll do it again, another attack. You haven't moved in your bed an inch.

Still beeping, still being filled, still being drained. I feel calmer just being right here next to you. It's a comfort. I can smell you despite the antiseptic surroundings, breathe you. I feel safe. I am at home, even though you lie there unresponsive.

I stay silent, cup your hands gently in mine, afraid I might break you. I keep looking at your body, dumbfounded at how things have changed so dramatically in the past twelve hours or so. My head is all over the place, scrambled, and my foot is total agony. It's all a monumental mess. I try desperately to block out our attack, yet keep playing the "what if" scenario. How things could have been so much different.

If only we hadn't gone to that damn Christmas ball. We had three party nights on the trot organised. It all sounded so exciting when we booked it back in November, but the thought of three nights out one week before Christmas filled you with dread. I should have read the signals. You didn't want to go that Friday, nor to the other parties the following two nights. You were just not in the mood. You told me you were knackered, chasing your end-of-year targets.

I'd noticed you'd been on edge, twitchy, snapping at me and the girls for the slightest thing. I teased you, said that you were no spring chicken anymore. Maybe it was the wrong thing to say. I was only joking. I had caught you a couple of times taking your mobile into the bathroom, heard you on the phone talking late at night. I was suspicious. Were you having a fling? I knew you were under pressure, you'd mentioned that two large sales had fallen through that week. December was historically a difficult time of year: your wealthy clients were too busy buying presents, spoiling their families, not buying expensive Ferraris, Bentleys and Rolls Royces.

The girls were beyond excited. They'd finished for

the school holidays. The house was filled with Christmas decorations, every room with a different theme. We were all set. I'd had my nails done at The Nail Studio and my hair blow dried at Zane's. Louise and I had our secret Santa at the wine bar that lunchtime. I was well into the Christmas spirit.

I was insistent, though, wasn't I? Excited as ever to dress up and party in Manchester. Excited to drink champagne, dance like crazy and live the high life. More than anything, I just wanted to cheer you up. We needed to spend some quality time together. In the past we always said the nights out we didn't want to go on were without doubt the best. I just wanted it to be like the old days again, just you and me. We had a cab booked to take us there and back, so neither of us had to drive. I was showered, dressed and was all set by the time you came home. As usual you rushed through the door and had ten minutes to get changed before the taxi arrived. You poured yourself a glass of wine, bringing it upstairs with you. You used to leave me your messages written on the steamy bathroom mirror—a heart with the words 'Love you, babe'—but just lately even that had stopped. God, it was irritating but it always made me smile. I could never wipe the bloody thing off. But there were no messages for me that night. I was convinced there was another woman, you were so distant and moody towards me. What was it? Why the mood swings?

We should have stayed in with our girls. We could have snuggled up and watched a film, *White Christmas*, our favourite, just the four of us. You and I would have been just as happy with a glass of wine or two.

We didn't need the weekend break either. What possessed me to bid for it? Our holidays were booked: Portugal, two weeks the following August; Quinta Do Lago, the same place every year. I know it was charity, it was just a bit of fun, but I got carried away though, didn't I? Too much champagne, swept away in the moment. If I hadn't raised my hand, not got so excited, we wouldn't be in this mess right now.

Look at you: unconscious, lifeless and it's all my fault. Our girls, hysterical wrecks, being comforted by your parents whilst I sit here feeling sorry for myself. The nurses arrive to turn you, to clean you up and check your drips and drains. It's time for me leave, to go back downstairs, back to solitary confinement, back to my haunting thoughts.

6

Jez

Twelve years ago

This wasn't exactly my goal in life. Burglary was never on my radar. I'd never stolen a single thing ever. For God's sake, when I was having my careers advice with old Percy at school, choosing me GCSE's, I never mentioned armed robbery to her. I s'pose you could say it was a case of wrong time, wrong place, an' a shed load of bad luck.

I'd led a pretty good life, thank you very much—to start with anyway. Living in the Pendle hills, old witch's country. Our big house was in the middle of nowhere, just my mum, dad, tosser of a brother, and my little sis. We had loads of land to get lost in I s'pose, a bloody great farmhouse with stables, great places to hide and get up to no good. I'd be up a tree all day long or smoking the odd fag down by the stream.

Yeah, so I went to a good school, an' it was the best one in the area. Didn't do me any good though, did it. I was an OK kid, straight A's until I was about fifteen. Then teenage years, spots, greasy hair, booze and girls got hold of me.

I always had a soft spot for the girls, I never failed in that department, had them queuing up. So I flipped. I bloody hated school and I couldn't wait to leave home, be on me own, bit of independence, get away.

My mum was alright, down to earth, "salty", as we say up north. She was good to us. So what that after tea she would down a glass or two of red wine, that was her little habit, but by the time I was fifteen she defo had a bit of a problem. I blame the old fella for that, the bastard, he treated her like shit; me and him, we hated each other. She was always on my side though, and sometimes she took a slapping for it too. I s'pose that's why she was always pissed. In the end, the more she drank, the worse it got—especially for me.

I hated my Dad, he was a complete tosser. He was an up-his-own-arse businessman, the big 'I am'. We clashed all the time. He practically disowned me, called me lazy, rude, a cocky little shit. So I fought back, I rebelled. My school results suffered big time. I blamed him for Mum being a pisshead. My big brother was high up in the army. He left home at seventeen—Golden Balls—he escaped. I had a lovely little sister though, who was just like my mum. We all loved little Sophie.

With below average A levels, I was never going to make it into uni, was I? So I applied for jobs. I found myself a decent little job in retail. Before long, was offered a junior management position in Manchester city centre. At last, I found my place. I was a bloody natural and couldn't wait to leave home, so when the Sales Director offered me the job, I jumped at the chance and moved out, as far away as I could. Things were on the up. I rented myself a great little flat on the outskirts of the city, nothing posh, a bit rough to be honest but it was near to my work and I could escape the control of my shit of a dad.

I was eighteen, I had my independence, and things were looking good. My new life was great. It didn't get much better than this. I could please myself: my life, my freedom, no rules, no bullying.

My cool one-bedroom flat had a tiny lounge, four units for a kitchen, a poxy little loo, but it had a massive double bedroom—somewhere to bring the ladies. I bought some second-hand furniture with the help of a couple of credit cards and not a bean from the parents. It didn't bother me if I never saw them ever again. My flat was pretty basic but at least it was mine, my own world with my own rules, no one telling me what to do. They never came to see me anyway, they didn't care. Only my little sister visited; she loved it. I miss her. Sophie was cool. She had brown hair, same as mine, but hers was long and wavy, and she had the same eyes as me. Sophie was defo the only reason why I had stayed at home for so long.

My new life was just right. I was on good money, I could go clubbing on a Saturday night, get pissed, and bring a bird back if I wanted. Now and then I would go for a beer in the pub with my mates, mostly neighbours from my flat. They were a great crack. I was living the dream, havin' the time of my life. It didn't get much better, not in my opinion anyway.

Working in the city was cool. For the first time in my life I was a happy lad. Brilliant at selling, I was a natural. I loved the buzz; there was nowhere better than Manchester.

A year later I was promoted, I had my own first shop. It wasn't massive, only small with six staff, a trendy menswear outlet just off the main high street. I was only nineteen, and some of my staff were old, twice my age, late forties. They cracked me up, 'specially when they told me personal stuff, shit about their other halves. I mean, as if I could give them advice. I knew nothing about that crap. I wasn't going to end up like my mum and dad, was I? Still, my staff all loved me. Why? I've no idea. They took the piss out of my wavy brown hair, they said I had lovely blue eyes. I was in good shape too, always at the gym in my spare time. Even at nineteen, I was pretty grown up. They all thought I was mid-twenties. They would work all hours for me. I was loved; they thought I was pretty cool. The ladies thought I was hot, so I even dated a few of them, didn't I!

The shop had been due to close because of crap figures over the previous two years, so I was there as an experiment to see if I could turn it around. I s'pose a young manager full of energy worked a treat. They were testing me out, seeing if I was up to the job. With recent figures so dire, sure, it could only go up. It was doable and I was the man to do it. So, from day one I used my charm, retrained bored staff, put a spark back into their dull old lives and my shop figures were on the up. My staff worked hard, and they loved working for me. I was a nice guy— well, at least I was back in those days.

7

Karen

Sunday May Bank Holiday 6.30pm

Please Will, its time you woke up now. I need you with me. I can't do this all alone, open your eyes, sweetheart. The twins want you back home, I want you home, back to the way we were before all this crap began. It kills me to see you lying there, surrounded by these damn machines, not a twitch from you. I need to let you know that I'm OK. He shot my foot but it's only a minor injury compared to yours.

My mind is racing but I daren't tell you anything whilst you're still unconscious. All I can do is think, think about us that night.

I couldn't see you, you'd fallen between the table and the worktop. I couldn't move. I thought you were dead, sweetheart. I'm trying not to relive it all but I just can't switch off.

I give your hand another squeeze, hoping for some kind of response, reassurance that you're going to be OK, that everything is going to go back to how we were, but still nothing, no sign of recovery.

When you didn't get up from the floor I literally froze, and that's when he pushed me towards the front door.

"Stay," I tried to say to Ellie and Jesse, their terrified faces peering at me from behind the door, but nothing came from my mouth.

The screams from our beautiful little girls faded as he dragged me away and there was nothing I could do; his gun was pushed hard against my throat. Tears streamed down my cheeks. My eyes blurred and it was difficult to see. Shaking hands fumbled with the keys as I struggled to start the car, my legs dead weights. My whole body quivered uncontrollably. I was convinced you were dead and my girls were all alone. Looking back, I'm sure my car lights weren't on for the first few minutes. The dashboard kept beeping, urging me to secure the seat belt. All my usual safety first thoughts were out of the window. I tried to focus, I tried to drive. It was a dense black night out there, the air still, heavy, and humid. The empty roads were narrow, winding and black, with no signposts, no direction. Minutes seemed like hours. I kept driving but I had no clue where I was headed.

Inside the car, the air was thick with his foul stench, making me wretch. It was difficult to breathe. I drove like a crazy woman. Where was I going? I had no idea Even though it was only a twenty-minute drive from home, I didn't know the area. You had driven us there that day. My heart was lodged firmly in my throat, gagging me. What was he going to do now? He'd said he was going to have me instead. What the hell did that mean? Rape?

My eyes were brimming with tears so it was impossible to see. How were our girls coping with you bleeding out on the kitchen floor? They don't know first aid; they're only ten, for God's sake, and they were stuck in the middle of nowhere. No one could have survived those gun shots, not at close range. Was he going back for the twins too when he'd finished with me? I kept imagining you motionless on the floor, blood everywhere, hearing those gunshots, a continual loop over and over. Where were we going? The guy stank—a combination of stale booze and cigarettes—making me feel sick. I felt filthy, petrified and very much alone.

The road ahead was haunting, dark with menacing trees seeming to grab towards me and the car. The monster next to me with his gun firmly against my throat. How I drove, I do not know. Finally, a junction, a road sign: Tarporley left, Crewe right.

"Left!" he screamed, pushing the gun harder into my neck. Any further and I was sure I would choke.

Christ! *Now what?* I kept hoping to wake up from the sick nightmare any moment. *Someone tell me it is a dream*, I kept saying to myself. *Wake up Karen, for fuck's sake, wake up!* Head muddled, my brain fried. Finally, there were lights ahead, a small village only one street long. *Please God, someone be there.* Was he going to kill me too? Would my girls be orphaned? There wasn't a soul around. Why would there be? The clock in the car said it was 02.20—everyone was fast asleep.

"OK, rich bitch, stop the car, get me your money." He stroked my face with the barrel of the gun. "Mmmmm, or shall I just have me a bit of rich first whilst I'm here." He grabbed a chunk of my hair, forced me towards him and tried to kiss me, his stale sweat-infested balaclava rough against my mouth. The stench of his breath made me gag, his disgusting fat tongue forced into my throat. In the past I've heard stories about women being attacked and thought I'd fight but I actually froze, couldn't speak, couldn't breathe and I couldn't move. He groped me with his left hand, keeping a firm grip on the gun with his other. "Not rich enough for you, am I? Scared little Karen," he laughed, mocking me as I managed to push him away.

"Cash point," he growled. "Get me your money."

I fell out of the car wearing just your jacket and shorts, barefoot, the road still warm from the evening sun. My card was snatched into the cash point. I punched the numbers.

INCORRECT PIN.

My mind blanked. "Shit!" I couldn't remember the bloody number. Fumbling with trembling hands, I tried again. Three cards, one after the other.

At last, the purr from the cashpoint, £250.

"Don't waste any more of my time. What's the fucking number, you stupid cow?" His face was directly next to mine.

"3750." He shoved our cards and our money firmly into his pockets then pushed me to the ground. Even behind that balaclava, I'll never forget those eyes, so full of hate and anger, just before he shot me.

The pain was so intense I almost blacked out, but I had to stay alert. Was he going back for my girls? He staggered towards my car, getting away. The door slammed, the gears crunched and the car screeched away. Silence—it was over. He was gone, but where to? Was he driving back to the cabin? Was he going back for Ellie and Jesse?

"Help me, someone," I tried to shout but my mouth was too dry. I couldn't speak, my ears ringing. Lights flicked on—they must have heard the shots—a few people ran out to help. "Call the police, call the police. He's gone to get my kids, Jeffries log cabin. He's killed my husband," I screamed like some crazed animal, vomiting with pain and terror. Then it all went black.

8

Karen

Sunday May Bank Holiday morning 3.00am

I guess I must have got to the hospital about fifteen minutes after you. When I came round, for a split second life was normal, until the terror of the night kicked in. It was chaos in the ambulance: bags, drips, blood, sirens. The pain in my left foot was excruciating, my head fuzzy. They must have given me gas and air or something. I was distraught about you, about my girls.

"Please, they are at Jeffries log cabins, somewhere in Delamere Forest. He's killed my husband and my girls are on their own. They're only ten. Get the police, please! What if he goes back and the girls are still there?"

"Karen, try to calm down. We have information that there is another ambulance just arrived at the hospital, a man with gunshot wounds."

"Is it him? Is he OK? What about my girls? Are they with him?"

"That's all we know right now. Let's sort you out first, OK? We're nearly at A&E."

The mask was placed firmly over my face. Yet again more gas and air, I guess, because it was making me dizzy.

The minutes dragged and it seemed like an eternity. I was rushed into the emergency room, I think. It's all so very hazy. I know I felt sick. I was terrified and I was shivering uncontrollably but I knew I had to stay awake. I had to make sure the girls were OK. I had to believe you were still alive. Outside the room, the police were waiting for me, ready to ask me questions.

"Please, where are my husband and my twins? I need to know how they all are."

I thought you were gone, Will. How could you have survived those gunshots at such a close range?

"Karen, try to stay calm. Your husband is here, and your daughters. They are all being seen to, they are safe. Now, we are just going to get this wound cleaned up. The police want to speak to you when you feel up to it. Try to stay calm, take some deep breaths. The quicker we do this, the quicker you get to see your family."

"Does anyone know if my husband is alright?" I kept prodding.

"He's had to go into emergency surgery, that's all we know for the moment."

My wound was bandaged and a large blue boot secured my foot, keeping things in place. They gave me stronger painkillers which made me light-headed. It was impossible to stay focused but I remember an X-ray was taken.

I had to stay composed so I would be able to talk to the police, but only managed to give a brief description of the events and the number plate of our car. I tried to give our bank details but he had taken our cards so that wasn't so easy. I could only give addresses in Manchester where we set up the accounts just in case he used them again. They'd explained how brave our girls had been. Without them, I don't think you'd be here. How they managed to stay calm and speak to the emergency services is beyond me. I am so proud of them.

"OK, if you remember anything else, Karen, please can you get back to me on this number."

The police officer left his card on the side table. I was alone in that room for a long time before Ellie and Jesse came bounding through the doors, eyes streaming, white, terrified faces.

"Mummy, Mummy!"

We hugged, we kissed and I couldn't let them go. Both girls squeezed in on either side of me and we just lay there holding each other. Thank God they were safe but we were still worried sick about you.

A porter wheeled me up to the orthopaedic ward and I was given a side room. The girls stayed with me for the rest of the night; they slept on camp beds donated from the children's ward. We were all restless throughout the night. None of us had much sleep.

When I woke up, for a split second all was calm until the dreadful events of the previous night kicked in. Again, disbelief, despair and questions—why? Why would someone do this to us? Everywhere ached like I'd been badly beaten. My foot had kept me awake all night, throbbing with sharp, stabbing pains each time I tried to turn over. The girls were still fast asleep, exhausted after their ordeal. They looked so calm, their innocent little faces so peaceful. I couldn't keep my eyes off them. On a hook on the side table hung the buzzer and I pressed it for some pain killers. I didn't want to disturb my girls so I placed my finger firmly against my lips to indicate to the approaching nurse not to make a sound.

"How are we feeling this morning, Karen?" she whispered.

"My foot is killing me, could I have some painkillers please?"

"OK hun, I'm just going to do your blood pressure,

temperature and pulse first then I will get you some medication. If you graded your pain from one to ten, what would it be?"

"Eight, ten? It feels like it's going to explode, it's throbbing all the time. Is there any news on my husband?"

"I'll get the doctor to come in and have a chat to you shortly, sweetheart." She was so lovely. Mind you, all of the staff have been pretty amazing.

The girls woke clambered on to my bed and clung tight to me, neither of them saying a word.

The nurse marked my chart then silently left the room. She was back within minutes with a glass of water and a small plastic tub of much-needed pills. I would have taken anything to blot out the past twenty-four hours.

The surgeon arrived shortly after Jesse and Ellie had fallen back in a deep sleep.

"Hello Mrs Keele, I'm Mr Rivers." He spoke quietly.

"Please, Karen, call me Karen."

"Let me tell you about your gunshot wound first then I will explain to you about your husband's condition." I wasn't bothered about me. My foot was painful, I'd been shot, I knew that. I just wanted to know about you. "You have been a very lucky lady indeed with the bullet as it went almost completely over your foot. It has fractured the tips of two metacarpals, but there's no long-term damage. Hopefully you should be out of hospital in the next few days. We will keep an eye on it in out-patients so it doesn't become infected. You will be on crutches for the next few weeks. A bit of physio and you should be back to normal in the next few months. No driving for six weeks though, OK?"

"OK, thank you. So how is my husband? How's Will?"

"Your husband, I'm afraid, is a completely different matter. He sustained a serious head injury which resulted in a swelling on his brain, so the next 24 to 48 hours are crucial. We have done a scan and there has been a bleed.

It doesn't look like we need to operate but we do need the swelling to go down. On top of that he also lost a serious amount of blood from his wound, three-and-a-half pints approximately. He has since had three emergency blood transfusions. With three gunshot wounds in his leg we've had to operate and he has been in surgery now for six hours. I'm afraid we couldn't save it. We had to amputate his leg above the knee this morning," he whispered discretely as he was well aware of the girls, who were still in a deep sleep. "His recovery will be a lot longer than yours, but first the swelling needs to reduce from his brain. It's going to be a long process and an awful lot of physio—that's of course when he eventually wakes up. Not only will he have to adjust to a new way of life physically, but he will need psychological help as well. Can I also recommend that you take full advantage of our counselling experts, for all your family? You've been through such a dreadful trauma."

I heard his words but I couldn't speak. Uncontrollable tears washed my face. The ball of tissues in my hand was soaked. What were we going to do?

"I will leave you alone for an hour, Karen, let the painkillers kick in. Then, if you like, we can wheel you up to intensive care so you can sit with your husband."

If you did wake up, what kind of life will it be for all of us? My injury by comparison seemed so trivial. I tried to muffle my sobs so as not to wake the girls. Eventually, the tablets must have kicked in and I was asleep.

9

Jez

He hated me from day one, the complete tosser. I thought
a few times if he'd treated me just a little bit better, how
my life would have been different—and his, eventually. I
wouldn't have done a ten-year stretch and he'd still have his
life. Jesus, I hope he is alive, otherwise I'm going down for
a serious amount of time. He did look pretty grim when I
left him lying on that floor. I had to check on the news on
the TV and radio—someone must be reporting it.

Will forced me to take on Jeanie, his bitch of a niece, to
work Saturdays. In fact, he'd been a total shit to me from
day one. I wasn't stupid, me and my staff knew Jeanie was
put there to keep an eye on us, to report back to Will, who
was my area manager. To begin with I couldn't stand her,
and neither could my staff. She was a right little smart arse,
far too young for the job. Nothing like the other girls in
the shop. Most of them were fit—even some of the over
forties weren't bad. So I'd had a few flings with my girls.
Who wouldn't? To them I was a god, for Christ's sake! But

49

I realised very quickly that mixing business and pleasure was not a good idea. I took my job very seriously and it had paid off, back in the day. I was proud of my position and I worked bloody hard at it. At last in my life, this was something I was good at.

They told me Will thought I was a right cocky little shit and should never have had this job, that according to him I was way out of my depth. Will couldn't understand why the sales director had given me this shop so young. It made no difference how well I did, he'd drag me down without fail, he'd put me in my place, bring me back down to earth. He gave me a proper hard time in that shop, took the piss out of my management, always trying to show me up in front of my staff. I don't think he was that good at his own job, he'd not been an area manager for long either. He was just like my dad, an absolute tosser. Even though my shop figures were on the up from the year before, week on week, he couldn't wait to find something wrong. Nothing was good enough for him, was it? There was always something for him to have a pop at; either the clothing wasn't set out to his liking or my window display wasn't up to scratch. He'd even lay into my staff if they weren't smart, nothin' was good enough. Basically, he wanted to make my life a total misery, and he did just that. He had someone else lined up for my job from day one and wanted me out on my ear. My sales manager, on the other hand, he was a top bloke, he was more interested in his figures. As far as he was concerned I was OK. I was doing a great job with a place that was sinking way before I got my hands on it. I was new, fresh, a rising star. My sales manager had big ideas for me, I was going places, and meanwhile Will, the tosser, well he bloody well hated it, didn't he!

Jeanie, from day one, had been a total pain in the arse. She was spoilt, idle and above it all. The staff nicknamed her 'Half-a-job Jeanie' because the loos and the kitchen were always dirtier after she cleaned them—that was when we could get her to lift a finger. She drove me up the wall; she was late every single day despite me being on her back. It was pretty bloody obvious she didn't want to be there either. Basically, we were babysitting her we all knew it. She was a fifteen-year-old stuck up madam. The staff knew from the off that they would be carrying her for until the day she decided to move on. My hands were tied; there was no way I could ever get rid of her, was there? She swanned around in her designer gear courtesy of rich parents and acted like she owned the joint, always angling her way out of work and flirting like mad with the wealthy looking punters in the hope of a sale. Jeanie was my worst salesperson; she was forever on her phone. She bought out the worst in me, and she was the only member of staff I had to nag.

My shop was top in the area, thank you, and had been there for twelve weeks in a row. No one could touch me and Will hated it. He told my staff I was a right little prat, and was way too young to have such a senior position. He'd wanted one of his older cronies to take it over, but its success was down to my charm and my hard graft. The staff loved me; I worked them hard and I made it fun. They loved coming to work, they told me loads of times.

Eleven months in and Christmas was well on its way. The yearly do was being organized by Lisa, my gorgeous full-timer. She was fit. We were going to our favourite Italian restaurant, Gino's, on December sixteenth at six, straight after work. The staff were buzzing. Jeanie was going too, which royally pissed off the others, me included, but we had no choice. If we'd stopped her, no doubt the tosser would have been on my back for that as well.

December was a total nightmare but good for business. Every day we were heaving. I had to work hard to motivate me staff, giving them ideas to sell well and increase the figures. It was our most profitable time of year and we had to make it big. I set them targets and they rose to it — they were all bloody brilliant. The atmosphere was electric. The music was trendy and loud, and the young kids hung out there. My shop was the place to be. The staff had decorated the shop with thick red tinsel, loads of lights and a huge Christmas tree. The window display was way over the top: massive green and red baubles, and hundreds of streamers, so many that you just about see through it, but it caught your eye on the high street. All was going well. It had been a bloody knackering week that seemed to go on for ages. Two people had been caught nickin' and I banned them from the shop. I couldn't bring myself to involve the police that close to Christmas; I guess in those days I was a bit of a nice guy, a bit soft. Not now though, am I, not after a ten-year stretch.

Saturday came. None of us got to take a full break and we just grabbed five minutes here and there. We were buzzing and looking forward to a bloody good night out, to let our hair down, get pissed and have a laugh. We gave it one hundred and ten percent.

Thank God six 'o' clock came, and the doors were finally closed. We had a twenty-minute turnaround to get the shop ready for Monday—the sale was going on the next week. I cashed up. Our figures were £2675 up on the same week last year, crackin' news. Yet another top week—we'd smashed it!

I'd put aside a few bottles of fizz to chill nicely in the fridge, waited until everyone was ready before I cracked them open. I toasted them all. I was proud. They looked pretty cool, all dressed up and ready to get pissed and hit the town. We'd never been on a night out together before. Jeanie had slapped on some false eyelashes, shedloads of heavy makeup on her massive blue eyes and now looked a hell of a lot older than her age. She was hot and she knew it, the little bitch. She'd curled her long blonde hair and wore a tight little red sparkly dress that showed off her cracking figure—size ten I guess—a right little tease. She was a bloody stunner and she loved it. All my staff had gone for it too and they all looked good, even the old forty-year-olds. The stock room stunk like a tart's boudoir. There was makeup piled on every surface, the stench of cheap hairspray everywhere and mirrors balancing from coat hangers. It was bloody chaos!

"Come on you lot, let's go party. Neck it back."

We'd warned her not to overdo it; no one wanted to babysit, especially with her being under eighteen.

"I can handle myself. I do this all the time," she bragged. Silly little cow.

Lisa had done herself proud though, she'd booked us a crackin' little meal at an Italian on Deansgate. That night had been a bloody good laugh. We stuffed ourselves with pasta, pizza, garlic bread, and olives. We'd drunk shedloads of beer and wine and finished with vodka shots. At eleven o'clock most of the oldies had had enough, but we were all pretty smashed. We took the piss out of them, the bloody lightweights. It was time for them to go, leaving a few of us stragglers behind: me, Jeanie, Ralph and Karen. Jeanie was becoming a right pain in the arse, hangin' around with men twice her age at the bar, little tart, she would easily have passed for twenty-one that night.

"I think we need to rescue those guys from a future prison sentence and get her in a cab home, Jez," Ralph stressed. "She's not far from you, can't you share a cab with her get her home?"

"Fuck off, Ralph, I'm not her nursemaid."

In the end, though, we had to prise Jeanie away from two pissed blokes old enough to be her dad and chuck her in the back of my cab. Shit, little did I know my nightmare had only just begun. She threw up all over her dress and my trousers. I was panicking. If she went home in this state, her old fella would go ballistic and blame yours truly and my staff for getting her so drunk. The taxi driver went nuts and threw us both out on the street. I took her back to my place, an attempt to sober her up. The plan was to get loads of coffee down her neck and get her back into another cab, send her on her way. At least that was my intention anyway.

I practically held her up all the way to mine. She was hammered and she threw up again, in the road this time, thank God. When we got to my flat, I tried wiping the puke from Jeanie's dress and my trousers, then sat her down. She absolutely stunk. I got myself changed, put the coffee on and made her drink it and water, gallons of the stuff.

She'd been at my place for at least an hour and I was getting more and more pissed off with her, plus I was knackered. It had been a long day. I let her sleep it off for a while then decided it was time she was off. I'd had enough. Thank God we hadn't left her behind though, anything could have happened, we would have been royally in the shit. She was totally off her face, clearly not used to booze, as she'd bragged earlier. I grabbed her shoulders and gave her a shake, plied her with another coffee. I wasn't expecting the next sentence; she totally threw me.

"Jez, I'm so sorry. Please don't tell my uncle; he'll tell my mum and dad and they'll go ballistic. I promised I wouldn't do this again."

I had to laugh. I'd never seen this side before; she was actually nice.

"Oh great, so you do this all the time, do you?"

"Listen, I know I've been a lazy bitch at work. I don't mean to; I just don't get along with adults. I've always had nannies, babysitters, tutors. My parents don't want to know. They dote on my little sister. It's like I don't exist. Dad will have a fit if he knows I've been like this again. Please don't tell on me."

I felt a bit sorry for her, to be honest. "You know, if you're nice to people, Jeanie, you might find they'll be lovely to you too. Give it a go sometime. I'll do you a deal:

you give it a try at work next weekend and I won't tell your uncle you were rat-faced. Promise me, next Saturday, OK? And I bet you'll see a difference with the staff. Come on, let's get you out of here."

"Thanks Jez."

She turned, put her hands on my hips and kissed me hard. It set me off. Bloody hell, she was good.

"Jeanie, stop it, leave off!"

But she didn't though, did she. Jeanie carried on. She was all over me. Before I knew it, our clothes were off and we were both in my bed. I couldn't resist. I'd had a skinful, she was gorgeous. I was weak, I was stupid. What can I say?

An hour later I was in my kitchen, gobsmacked, my head in my hands, wondering what the fuck I had done. This was not my plan. She, on the other hand, had a bloody great smile on her face.

"I hope you're not regretting anything, Jez. I've had a great night, have you?"

"Are you nuts?"

I was fuming with her, yet she was pretty cute. She kissed me once more and Christ, we were at it again, different room this time. She was a fit little thing and she knew exactly what she was doing. I couldn't keep my hands off her. Still, when it was over and I'd come to my senses, I was shittin' myself. I grabbed her clothes up from a pile on the floor and threw them at her.

"You'd better get dressed! Your uncle will sack me if he doesn't chop my balls off first."

"He doesn't give a shit about me. You like me though, don't you Jez?"

I grabbed her by the arm. "Come on, you're out of here. Let's get you home."

I took her downstairs, called a cab, threw her in it and then went back to my flat, poured myself a massive brandy and just stared at the wall. Jesus, what the fuck had I done?

What the bloody hell had I done? Think I downed a few more brandies then I must have collapsed, I was out of it.

When I woke up on Sunday I had the mother of all hangovers, my head was banging and my mouth was like the bottom of a bird's cage. I just sat there most of the day. She was doin' my head in. I needed to check her application form in the morning, check her age, hope to God she wasn't still fifteen. She'd been with us eleven months so she must have turned sixteen but I just didn't remember her having a birthday. Why had I been such a twat? I hated myself too. I couldn't stop thinking about how gorgeous she was, and so mature. I bet she'd had a few blokes before me, she seemed to know what she was doing. If I was honest, I couldn't wait to see her the next week. I sat there all day Sunday, just thinking about me an' her in *my* bed over and over. Scared shitless and excited at the same time. The day dragged. As much as I tried to forget the night before, that tape played over and over again in my head, me and her at it in my bed. Christ, she was four years younger than me. Just how old was she? I hoped she'd had her sixteenth birthday since she started with us. First thing tomorrow morning I was checkin' her file. Her uncle and her dad would both defo kill me. My career in retail was well and truly over.

First thing Monday morning I was in the staff room looking for Jeanie's application form. My hands were shaking, trying to open her folder. I just needed to see it for myself in black and white. I'd made a strong coffee, knocked it back and ran me finger down the page, to the date of birth. Oh my God, sixteen next birthday, only four weeks away. In a court of law, your honour, I was a fucking paedo!

That week was so bloody slow, probably the longest week of my entire life. As the days dragged towards Saturday, I couldn't wait to see her. For one, she needed to keep her mouth shut, and two, I wanted the whole thing to happen all over again. I couldn't get enough of her. I was shittin' myself that any minute her uncle would come in and kick the livin' daylights out of me ... or, even worse, her dad would pay a visit. He was one tough mother. I was paranoid. I got the impression that all the staff knew too. What a twat I'd been! But I couldn't get her out of my head. Despite trying not to, I kept reliving Saturday night and couldn't wait to see that fit little bod of hers again. She was an absolute cracker. Even though she was younger, she knew exactly what she was doing. Jeanie was all I could think about. No one had made me feel this good before, but she had to keep her gob shut, that was for sure.

Saturday came at last and in she came. She was full of it. From that day onwards she'd changed: she became a valued member of my staff, and turned out to be a great little sales girl. She even had a good sense of humour once you got to know her, the stroppy teenager was gone. The staff began to like her. "What the hell's changed, Jeanie?" they kept asking. She was co-operative and she'd do anything for me. I had her wrapped around my little finger—or at least I thought so. Overnight, she'd become a great little worker, a complete transformation, and great fun to be with.

Jeanie and I were starting to get it on, in secret of course. The staff teased me. They weren't stupid, they knew she had a bit of a thing for me. What they didn't realise was it was a two-way thing. "You really are going to have to cool it at work," I told her, "they know you like me."

"And how about you, Jez? I know you like me too." She knew she had me.

10

Karen

Monday May Bank Holiday 10.30am

I must have dozed off. Your drip monitor jolts me back to life. It must have been going off for a few minutes as the nurse is already changing the bag over. She has a flick though your notes, gives me a polite nod and leaves. You look so peaceful. I wanted to tell you about our little girls. Those kids have been me absolute rock for me, with you up here. They're so worried about you.

Ellie and Jesse were either side of me when I woke up this morning. Your parents were busy with the doctors. They were both holding my hands, bless them. Their little eyes were brimming with tears and I had to bite hard on my bottom lip to stop myself from losing it.

We were interrupted by the nurse carrying a loaded tray. It was a good distraction

"I put some extra cakes and biscuits on for you. Try to eat something, ladies." They were so kind but I just couldn't eat a thing. The last thing I fancied was food.

The girls picked at their cakes, only managing a couple of small bites each, hardly touching their orange. I drank half a cup of tea, but even that seemed to stick in my throat.

"Mummy, how are you, and how is Dad? When can we go to see him?"

"Dad is in a very special ward at the moment, where the doctors and nurses can give him all the care that he needs. He's lost an awful lot of blood but he's OK, thanks to you two. You both were so brave, you saved his life. I'm so, so, proud of you," I kissed both foreheads and wiped their tears with the back of my hand, not knowing quite how to tackle the head injury and amputated limb explanation. "Dad is very poorly at the moment, but they have said that I can see him this morning. Let me go up first, find out how he is then maybe we can all see him tomorrow together. How does that sound?" We squeezed each other tight. I couldn't let them go. "How are you both?" Even at the age of ten, they seemed to have grown up fast. Ellie, being the eldest, had taken on a protective role. She kept pulling the blanket over us and stroking our heads. Jesse, our baby of the family, still insisted on sucking her thumb and playing with a long strand of her hair. The difference in them was more obvious with her being the smaller of the two.

"The lady on the phone said we were very grown up, Mum."

"You were, sweetheart, I'm very proud of you both."

Their blonde curls were stuck to their faces as their tears kept coming.

"We didn't know where we were."

"The lady told us to see if a big book was on the table, with an address inside. How did she know that?"

"Usually holiday homes have an information book. That lady sounds very clever to me."

"She was."

We snuggled together and do our best to watch some cartoons on the TV. I literally couldn't let them go.

"I know you'd be so proud of these girls," I whisper as I stroke your hair back and kiss your cheek before I leave. Still no movement from you. I am so exhausted today, desperate to lie down and close my eyes. It's time for me to go back downstairs to be with our twins.

11

Monday May Bank Holiday 2.00pm

Your parents have taken Ellie and Jesse back to ours to give them a change of scene and attempt to feed them. So now I am alone. The video plays, but this time I'm wondering why you took so long to come out into the kitchen. Why you left me there for ages, knowing full well I was naked with some madman brandishing a gun. It just didn't make any sense. OK, you turned up eventually, but to me that seemed like a lifetime. There are questions I need to ask you. Questions I hope one day I get the chance to ask you.

My brain's on overload trying to think back, and quite frankly it's wearing me down. I'm completely shattered. I do manage to drift off though, and I dream we are in Quinta Do Lago at Julia's, our favourite beach bar, for lunch. I order a vodka iced tea and you have a large beer. When our drinks finally arrive, they are so huge that they are impossible to lift. It is an unbearable 98 degrees plus and the sun is beating down overhead. We are roasting.

To make matters worse, there are no umbrellas for shelter so no escape. Even though it is August, the bar staff play Bing Crosby's White Christmas and everyone else in the bar has hats and coats on except us. I'm wearing the skimpiest bikini and you have the most hideous budgie smugglers on. Both our outfits are grossly unflattering and people all around us are laughing and pointing. It is humiliating. Within minutes, our skin is blistering and the girls are screaming from the shoreline, but the sea is now miles away and we can't get to them. The sun is scalding my foot and you still have your drip bags…

I hear a trolley crashing through the door, but there is no door. The bartender is wearing an undersized nurses outfit which is splattered in dark dried bloodstains.

I wake sweating and screaming for Ellie and Jesse. I am losing the plot. I'm back in my side ward.

"Please God!" I cup my head in my hands. My foot throbs under the covers.

The lunch trolley is at the foot of my bed, but with no bartender in fancy dress. Instead it's a very confused looking nurse. The good news is that the lunch trolley is soon followed by the drugs trolley and the much-needed pain relief. Are the drugs making me even more loopy? Possibly.

"How about you try to eat, Karen, and we'll take you back up to see your husband later. You need to be strong … for Will's sake, and your girls."

Just the smell of the gravy churns my stomach. The green beans are pushed slowly around the plate. I try a mouthful of mashed potato but even that seems to be lodged firmly in my throat. I can barely drink the tea, just managing a few sips, and a small tub of fruit yoghurt is the only food I finish.

The nurse leaves me with a toothbrush and a hairbrush so I try to smarten myself up. I don't want you to see me this way, just in case you should wake up. Zane only put the blonde streaks in three days ago, so I attempt to brush out the knots and put some waves back into my hair. I look like I'm wearing red eyeliner which is clashing with my hazel eyes. I look dreadful. My regulation dressing gown absolutely swamps me. I'm guessing it's a size sixteen plus as I can almost wrap it around me twice over.

A different porter arrives this time and takes me back up to intensive care. I am still so embarrassed at my actions yesterday when I tried to wake you.

Before I go back in, the head nurse wants to tell me about your progress. "Karen, hi, I just wanted to update you about Will's condition. Good news, the swelling has gone down on his brain, his vital signs have improved. Everything has gone as well as could be expected. He is still on morphine and hasn't opened his eyes yet. We will keep him in intensive care for at least the next twenty-four hours then, when we are happy with his progress, he'll be moved to the surgical ward, hopefully in the next few days."

"That's brilliant news, thank you. I'll tell his parents."

"Not to worry, we can do that for you if you like."

"Thank you so much."

I can stay for a good couple of hours this time before the girls are due back. I desperately want to be here when you wake up, but you are still, no movement, no twitches, no squeezes from your hand. I'm just grateful that you are going to survive.

The porter pops his head around the corner to take me back downstairs and, just as I kiss you goodbye, your eyes flutter.

"Karen, Karen," you whisper. "How are you? Did he hurt you? Where are the girls? Did they catch the bastard? Why did he ... the prick ... are you hurt? I hate that ... Did you get the insurance?" You're rambling, in and out of sleep.

63

"Will, it's OK, I'm OK, we're OK. I'll do the insurance another time." You almost made me laugh. That's the last thing on my mind with so much else going on, but typical of you always thinking about the finances. "Yes hun, I'm here, calm down sweetheart. I love you so, so much." I stroke your hair back, run my hand down the side of your cheek, my attempt to pacify you. I'm desperate to hold you tight but still afraid I might break you.

"Love you too, babe," you whisper. "That bastard ..." Your voice trails off. "Can't believe ..." You drift into sleep.

"Can I stay a bit longer?" I ask the porter.

"Yes of course, love," he says. "Just tell the nurses when you want to go back down to the ward and they'll buzz me."

My hands are trembling. I can't quite believe it and I bolt out to the nurses' station to tell them the news. A couple of them follow me in, and torches again shine in your eyes as they ask you questions and try to get another response. I leave them to it and try to compose myself in the family room.

"Karen, you can go back in now. He's asking for you."

"Thank you." It's the first time I think I've managed to smile.

Your eyelids flutter and your entire body twitches, which clearly causes you pain, judging by your wincing.

"How are my girls, babe?" You're a bit more lucid this time.

"They are OK, hun. The police were very impressed with Ellie and Jesse; they saved your life. I can't believe how amazing they were." I ramble on but you've already fallen back into a deep sleep.

I'm by your side for another half an hour, too scared to leave you alone. You keep drifting in and out of consciousness. The nurses return once more to take your temperature and blood pressure, so I leave them to it.

"See you later, hun. I'll tell everyone you're awake." But you are already sound asleep.

I kiss your forehead then I am wheeled back down to my room. The porter chats all the way, but I hear nothing. At last you've come back to me.

Back in my room, the exhaustion hits me. I'm fighting to stay awake. The police have been waiting for me outside.

"Hi Karen, I'm DCI Graham, please call me Mike, and this is my assistant, DS Tracy Jarvis. We deal with armed robbery cases and have been assigned to your case.

They don't look a bit like police, both in jeans, T-shirts and baseball hats. He's a polar opposite to you, with cropped brown hair and smiling green eyes. He's a bit older than you as well, I guess about thirty-sevenish and he clearly works out. You'd be envious of his physique; you'd probably call him ripped or something like that. His partner, on the other hand, looks like a work experience candidate. She looks about twelve, thirteen, and she definitely hasn't had kids with her tiny frame. Bless her, the hat doesn't do her any favours either with large wisps of mousy blonde hair straggling at the base of the cap shielding small grey eyes void of any makeup. They have a few more questions to ask. Have I remembered anything new? Do we know anyone that might hold a grudge against us? Although they believe it was a random attack, an opportunist, they just need to check. They have found my car and it is now with forensics.

"We think we have someone on CCTV and as soon as we have a sharp image we will get back to you. We are so sorry to hear about your husband's leg."

"Thank you. We all have a lot of work and rehab to get through right now."

"And your kids, they were pretty amazing last night."

"They saved his life. They've gone home with Will's parents." Those girls have done us proud.

"Did they tell you about the phone call to the emergency service?"

"Not much. To be honest we've hardly said anything today. We're all still in shock."

"Here are some of the transcripts. You have two very bright little girls." Mike hands me a piece of paper.

Caller:	Daddy's dead, Daddy's dead!
	His leg.
	There's lots of blood, it's coming
	out of his leg.
Operator:	Where are you? Try to stay calm.
Caller:	We don't know, we don't know.
	Dad's dead! There's blood all over the
	ground. We are away with Mum and
	Dad in a log cabin.
Operator:	What's your name? How old are you?
Caller:	I'm Ellie, Jesse is my twin.
	We are both ten but I'm the oldest,
	and the biggest.
Operator:	OK, Ellie, tell Jesse to get something
	like a belt and tie it as tight
	as you can above where your
	Daddy's leg is bleeding.
	Can you find something like a book
	on the lounge table that might have
	the name of the cabin on it.
Caller:	Jesse is tying Daddy's belt around his leg.
Background:	(from the background) We are at Jeffries
	log cabin, Delamere Forest.
Operator:	Now, ask Jesse to get a clean towel and
	Ellie, you press it hard against where
	he is bleeding. Stay with him.
	Tell Jesse to switch all the lights
	on so we can find you easily, OK?
	The ambulance is on the way.

Mike explained that within minutes, sirens could be heard on the recording. To those poor girls it must have seemed like a lifetime. The ambulance crew had wrapped them both in blankets while they dealt with your bleeding.

"Well, they definitely saved his life. Without their quick thinking, I think we could have been looking for a murderer."

"Oh God!" I gasp. I wasn't expecting that. I am determined to control myself though, enough tears for one day. "Why would someone do this to us?"

Mike puts a reassuring hand on my shoulder. "Unfortunately, we don't know yet, apart from the burglary. All this is going to take time to heal." Wise words from an experienced man. "We'll call round again tomorrow if that's OK with you?" And with that, they were gone.

Once more I sit there stunned, still in total disbelief.

About seven thirty apparently, your parents came back to see me in my side ward. They have brought my toiletry bag, a nightdress and some new pyjamas for you, to try and make us both feel a bit more comfortable, a bit more at home. Whilst drifting in and out I sleep, I hear them whisper:

"Shhhh, let her rest for a while."

My eyes feel so heavy, I can't bring myself to open them, so I allow myself the luxury of falling back into a deep sleep. It's not without interruptions and I twitch and jump at the slightest sound in the room.

The girls have made a real effort and it breaks my heart. Ellie is in her favourite sparkly jeans and star top, the one you bought her for Christmas, and Jesse is wearing her cute little rainbow dress. How different they look from earlier—only the dark circles around their eyes gave away their sadness.

"They wanted to wear something bright and cheery," your mum whispers. "They've both had a bit of tea: fish fingers and chip butties. The nurses have told us the news; it's wonderful. We'll go up in a minute." Bless your Mum, her face is animated for the first time since this whole nightmare began and her huge eyes are glossy with suppressed tears.

"He woke up just as I was about to leave him, and he's spoken to me. To be honest, a lot of it didn't make any sense, but he's awake, that's the main thing."

"That's brilliant news, sweetheart."

"Flowers for you, Mum." Ellie placed a small bunch of daffodils from our garden on my bed.

"My favourite, thank you sweetheart."

"And chocolates. Nanny said you needed to eat too. Shall we try one to make sure they are OK?" Jesse makes me laugh, the chocoholic, just like you. Still, at least they were eating something.

"You and your dad are chocolate mad. Shall we save some for him when we see him later this week? Tuck in, ladies."

"Let me sort your pillows for you, hun." Your mum, ever the carer. She would have made a great nurse back in the day.

I sip some water. It's an effort to eat even my favourite nut cluster. Two sweets down and the girls' mood changes, reliving the horror of the previous 24 hours.

"They wanted to tell you about their phone call," your dad prompts.

"Yeah, the police were telling me how amazingly brave you both were. They were very impressed with you two."

"We phoned 999, Mummy, we thought Dad was dead," they both say in unison as if reading each other's minds.

"He was bleeding, there was lots of blood," Ellie recalls quietly.

"I had to stop the blood whilst Ellie was on the phone ... Daddy's face looked white, he didn't move."

"We thought he'd died." Jesse's huge eyes had filled as she relayed the story.

"A policeman was here earlier, he told me how brave both of you were, how you saved your Daddy's life. I'm so proud of you both ... and he was very impressed with you both."

"We tried to stop the blood. The lady on the phone told us what to do," Ellie adds. They both look so serious. "We didn't know where we were. We were so scared. We didn't know where you'd gone, Mummy," Ellie finishes her sentence, looking so much older than her sister.

Seeing them like this breaks my heart

"You did amazingly! And thanks to you two, your daddy is alive."

"Crying is good, girls, let it all out, let the hurt and shock come out," your mother says, and your dad gives her a nod. The girls sit and stare at the television on the wall, not really taking it in. Your mum whispers that they were like this at home and she could see them mulling the events over and over.

"When can we see Daddy?" Jesse turns towards me, her eyes pleading.

"Maybe tomorrow, let him rest tonight. He's still very weak."

"When will we be able to see him, Mum?" Ellie presses me for a more precise answer.

"I'll be with him later tonight, let me see how he is. We'll try for tomorrow if the doctors let us. He's still very poorly and it makes him very sleepy, so for now he needs a lot of rest, peace and quiet."

"Let's go, girls, and we can all get some rest." Your mother grabs her handbag and tries to usher them both from the room.

"Do we have to?" The twins cling to me tightly

and I reciprocate. I don't want them to go either. It is heartbreaking; selfishly, I don't want to be alone.

Left to my own devices it is impossible not to think that this time two days ago. Everything was perfect and we were all so happy. The horror of Saturday night comes back to me again. I sit, numbed, motionless. My foot is beginning to twinge again; I think it's time for more painkillers. I buzz for pills and hope the porter can take me back upstairs to be by your side for the last time today.

This time you are a bit more lucid. The night nurse has a chat with me.

"Does he know about his leg?" I ask.

"No, not yet. He's still on strong pain relief. I think tomorrow might be a good time to tell him."

"Can I be there with him when you explain?"

"Yes, that's a great idea. I think the surgeon was going to ask you anyway, it's best Will has all the support possible." She holds open the door for my wheelchair and places her hand on my shoulder, giving me a genuine, sympathetic smile.

I look up to the ceiling, try to hold back my tears, and move from the wheelchair to a seat so I can get nearer to you. With your hand cupped in mine, I count our blessings at how lucky we are that you're still here with us.

For a moment, you look at peace until your eyes flutter, your right hand twitches and a line indents on your forehead. Is it pain or stress? It's hard to tell.

"You going to be OK, babe?" you whisper.

"Love you, Will, love you so much." I'm so choked, it's all I can say and then the tears come.

"Don't cry. We will get through this, we'll be OK. Have they caught the bastard who did this to us?"

"No sweetheart, nothing yet." Tonight, for the first time since the incident, you seem to be a bit more awake. You talk for a few more moments, well, more babbling really. I'm guessing it must be the pain killers as you keep wandering off, distracted, giving me minimum eye contact. At least you don't mention your leg yet. I stay for another half hour, but you seem to be getting more tired, so it's best to let you sleep. It feels like the first time I've smiled all day. I buzz the nurse and within minutes the porter returns to take me back down to my room. I could do with some rest too, I'm totally exhausted. Sleeping tablets will be a good idea to take my mind off things.

I have a good six hours. When I wake up it is as if I've been hit by a train. I am dripping with sweat and there is someone in my room.

"He's back … Oh God, help me!" I snatch at my bed sheets. "Why don't you leave us alone!" I scream.

"It's OK, love," says a soft voice, the nurse at the end of my bed making notes.

I'm trying to catch my breath and calm myself down.

"I'm so sorry." The nurse hugs me. "It's OK, sweetheart. I'm sorry, I didn't mean to frighten you. Here, let me sort your pillows. Would you like a drink of water?"

The pain in my foot is unbearable and I'm drained. How much more can I take? She gives me more tablets and, before long, I am out cold.

They let me sleep and it's about 8.30ish when I came round. Although I've had a good night, my head is now hazy and groggy—I think it's the effects of the sleeping tablets. My foot is throbbing again. Saturday night is back in my head. Will these flashbacks and horrors ever go away? Breakfast arrives and I force some toast and marmalade down. It's the most I've managed to eat.

12

Karen

Tuesday 10am

You're asleep again when I get back up to intensive care. You look so peaceful, no stress, not a care in the world. That's short-lived though, for when you do wake a deep frown line burrows firmly on your forehead. You're a troubled man. It's going to be another long day.

"Have they caught him?" It's the first thing you say. "That bastard!"

You don't even say hello to me. Your mood is low, you're consumed with hate and you keep asking "Why?"

As you go round in circles with your ranting, my mind drifts off to Mum. When I really need her she's unable to help. I have made the conscious decision not to tell her. She'd only get distressed and forget moments later. It so it isn't worth the hassle.

Her condition has been getting progressively worse these last few weeks, especially since her fall, and I make a mental note to phone Jo, our secret weapon, to ask her to pop in and check on her. You know how vigilant I've had to be with her since losing Dad. She's only 65, for God's sake, far too young for this horrendous disease. I needed her to remain independent for as long as she possibly could, more for my own sanity. Putting her in a home had not been an option after she left hospital. The professional advice was not to move her into residential care until the later stages for fear it would accelerate the condition, increase her confusion. So that's why every week, much as you hated it, I did my duty, the thirty-mile round trip to check on her. Although she wasn't too bad then with her confusion, she still needed my help. At least now I can put my hand on my heart and know I tried my best. The times I would stand in that car park outside her apartment, bags brimming to the top with her weekly shop. I knew it was a thankless task. I knew full well that all would be forgotten by the time I arrived back home; she'd assume she'd bought the shopping and that she'd kept the house clean. I was knackered. God knows you pointed that out to me enough times. I would tidy, I would change the soiled sheets, I would sort out the washing and cook her something nutritious to eat, and bless her, Mum believed she did all of it herself, she believed she was coping just fine. I honestly don't know how I did it, to then come home to you and the kids and start all over again. The whole process drained me. I was racked with guilt, still am if I'm honest, and there was no quality mother and daughter time.

When social services scheduled to drop in now and then, looking back it was a complete waste of time. She was so forgetful she'd refuse to let them through the door, she couldn't remember them. All those poor care workers that would attempt to go in just to administer her drugs, unsuccessfully. I never realised just how proud and stubborn she was until then. Even her meals on wheels were refused entry in the end. From our point of view, it would have been another person seeing her in the daytime, but it fell flat on its face when she refused to let them in. Wasn't she a nightmare, bless her.

"I'm not wasting any more money," she'd complain. "I don't like the bloody food; I'm not letting them in." She made me laugh sometimes, through all the heartache.

We got away with Jo though, didn't we–our secret cleaner lady. Everyone needs a Jo. Poor Mum, the lies we told her for our own sanity, saying Jo was an old friend of mine, that we'd worked together years ago, bribing her way into Mum's house each week with a cake and a coffee. How deceptive we were. Jo would say, "You sit down, Mary, and I'll make us both a brew." Meanwhile, she cleaned the kitchen and tidied around. They would have coffee and a chat, and Jo would ask to use the loo, giving her a bit of time to quickly wipe around the bathroom. Still, at least Mum could remain a proud lady, have her house cleaned and be none the wiser.

Online Tesco's shop was a top idea every week too, not that Mum would eat any of it. The times I emptied her fridge the following Saturday with out-of-date food, mouldy bread or gone-off milk. I'm surprised she didn't suffer from stomach upsets.

Still, all you and I wanted was more visitors for Mum throughout day, meaning we could rest assured she wasn't spending too much time alone, for our own sakes as well as hers. I think we did get some success from our lies, even if she didn't always let people in. In hindsight, in Mum's world these people were strangers to her, with her dreadful memory thanks to her illness.

How did anyone expect her to remember to take her tablets that were delivered weekly from the pharmacy in organized dosette boxes? She couldn't remember anything ten minutes previously, let alone a day's worth of pills. Looking back, it was a bit ambitious to get her to take them. I shouldn't laugh, but when I saw the spare bedroom had become a dumping ground for the tower of unused tablets, boxes untouched and piled high neatly on the spare bed, I had to smile.

Still, we knew it was only going to get worse though, didn't we? Maybe one day there will be a cure—too late for Mum though. I hated the way people interpreted the illness, saying 'oh, they've lost their marbles', or 'they are mad, going barmy/loopy/stupid.' It was so unfair. It is such a misunderstood, undignified and cruel way to end the last years of your life. If I'd told my friends my mum had cancer or heart disease, they would have said, "Oh God, poor you, your poor mum!" But sadly, the minute you mentioned Alzheimer's there was always an embarrassed silence, a lack of understanding.

I felt for Mum though, the times she'd become distressed with her mind playing its cruel tricks on her. I was convinced she was hallucinating. Being the only one left, I bore the brunt of her confusion and frustration. "Where's my purse?" was a familiar upset that had us turning the house upside down in earlier years. "Someone's stolen my jewellery!" was another. Frequent trips to the bank, as she would forget she had been there the day before. Trying to pay several times for the milk and the papers was a frequent occurrence. Thankfully they had all gotten used to her; thank God they were all honest. "Your mum's tried to pay me three times this week," I would get from George the milkman. He had known her for a while and he was the same age. He told me once that he felt so sorry for me. Another one Mum would do was in the winter as the dark nights settled in, she would go off to bed at 5.30 pm thinking it was later. Then at 2.30 in the morning she'd be on the phone to me, scolding me for being out too late. These things had taken their toll on you and I for some time now.

There was no point telling her about the attack. I don't have a spare moment anyway; I'll be in hospital for at least a few days. I'll get Jo to check in on her.

13

Jez

Sunday May bank holiday 10.40pm

I've no clue how the hell I drove that car through those dark country lanes, totally stoned and off my face. I know I abandoned it in some waste ground near Crewe train station. Should of set fire to it, thinkin' back, but my head wasn't straight, was it? My prints would be all over it by now. I lit my last spliff and tried to calm down. Now I had his money, his cards and her mobile. Still pissed and sweating like a pig, even I could smell my own BO and booze. Jesus, I stunk. I couldn't believe what a total prick I'd been. I'd shot them both, for fuck's sake. I had to get my head straight. To start with, I needed to stop smoking this shit and get away fast. I couldn't get Karen out of my head though. Christ, she looked so fucking good. I hadn't been near anyone in the buff since Jeanie, and that was ten bloody years ago.

At Crewe, I must have staggered around a bit; all I do know is I had the sense to catch the next train to Manchester. Practically fell into my seat by the window and couldn't stop the vision of Karen's fit little bod getting into my head. OK, I needed to get away but I wouldn't half mind one more look at her. She made me well horny and I'm sure we had a moment. There was something in her eyes, a little look she gave me. She was a top bird in that oversized jacket of his, classy, just how I like 'em. OK, so I didn't get a proper kiss but I'm sure there was a bit of a spark there, a bit of a connection. Think she liked being with a man for a change. I mean, I've never struggled in the ladies department before, have I? If I was to meet up with her she wouldn't recognise me anyway, thanks to my balaclava. She'd be clueless. I'm a good lookin' bloke, a damn sight better than that tosser she's married to.

Anyway, back to earth, Jez. Need to figure out my next move. What the fuck had I done? There was no way I going back inside again, no way. The drugs and drink kicked in and I reckon I must have passed out. I vaguely remember the train guard waking me to pay for a ticket (the twat), which I paid, thanks to the cash from the tosspot and his wife. When the train stopped at Manchester, the guard nudged me again.

"Come on, mate, it's the end of the line, time to go home."

I staggered back to my halfway house. How the hell I found it, Christ knows. My head was all over the place. Why did I have to shoot them? That was not in my plan. I was only supposed to rob them both, not shoot, for fuck's sake. I had to get him back though, call it closure. It was over, my life was over, for real this time. I had to get out sharpish, but Karen was seriously messing with my head. With the help of her phone, maybe I could get to her place and see her just one more time. It was doable. Maybe she'd come with me, get away from that knob.

I'd spent ten years of my life at Her Majesty's pleasure,

Strangeways, thanks to Jeanie, the little bitch. I blame him for that as well. She wouldn't have got the job if I wasn't over a barrel to take her on. He stitched me up well an' truly with that one, didn't he!

We'd been together on the quiet for six months. She made it pretty obvious at work and was starting to be a right bloody nuisance. I was shit scared and she knew it. The staff must have known something was going on, they weren't stupid. Dawn, my supervisor, had warned me a few times to watch my back, but by then it was too late. I was in too deep and I was nuts about her. Even though she was only sixteen, she wore the trousers. After a few months, she even started to demand more money. She kept on about a promotion, little bitch. Jeanie was great at work with everyone else, but as time went on I guess she was blackmailin' me. She threatened me a few times, and joked about me bein' a paedo—could of strangled her that night. We'd both been on the piss an' she blurted that one out. It got to the point I couldn't think straight or function. She played some serious games with my head. The shop figures were falling and I was on the edge. It all came to a head when she let it slip she was pregnant.

"What? Well, I'll pay for you to have an abortion!"

I could have killed her. I couldn't believe what I was hearing. She was so cool about the whole thing. She sure as hell wasn't expecting my reaction

"I'm having this baby," the little tart insisted. "You can't make me get rid of it, and don't even think about dumping me. I'll tell my uncle you've been after me from day one. Ha, you could end up on the sex offenders list. I was underage, remember!"

I was gobsmacked. "You absolute cow! That's not funny, Jeanie ... listen to me. We are too young for this shit. You are too young for a kid!" I screamed. "You're nuts, you're fucking nuts! Your uncle won't just sack me, he'll bloody kill me." I poured myself a large one and just got wasted.

She was so used to getting her own way, spoilt little bitch, and I honestly believe she thought she'd got me. I reckon she thought that I would come round sooner or later. We needed to move on this one quick if she was to get rid of it—once I was sober that was. I got through most of a bottle of brandy that night and I slept like a log. She told her parents she was staying at her mates, so I was stuck with her all day. She was under the impression things were going to be all cosy. She was well out of order. I suppose Jeanie was thinking she'd move straight into my place. Yeah, like that was going to happen. We'd have this little baby, and I'd work my arse off. She'd have somewhere to play house. She had it all planned, except she'd not planned for my reaction. My life was all goin' so well, why did it all go so wrong?

She was basically a rich bitch from a posh background. Jeanie had done her time at a very expensive boarding school and had zero quality time with her parents except Christmas and Easter. She hated school, just like me. Jeanie was only interested in number one and boys, so when it came to sixth form she didn't make that either. Her GCSE results were even worse than mine, so the school wouldn't take her back on to do her A levels under any circumstances. She'd been working Saturdays at my shop for about eleven months. If Jeanie did have any ambition in life it was to be a model—which she could have done, to be fair, she was a stunner. So, when the shop job came up, her dad had persuaded his brother to take her on. It gave her the chance to work for a living. Her parents stopped her allowance, which made her get out and earn her own money. But Jeanie was above it all, wasn't she! She'd never even hoovered in her life or cleaned a toilet at home, let alone our staff loos. These things were beneath her. At home, they had staff to do those shitty little jobs.

A few weeks into dating she'd told me she had her eye on me from day one, although I was too thick to pick up on it. She'd dreamt of all sorts of different scenarios—me an' her alone somewhere in the shop, maybe in the stockroom after hours. All she craved was someone to love and to love her back. I guess with this little baby, to her it looked like the real deal, a cosy little life. I was doing well, wasn't I! Had a good job, had a flat all ready and furnished for her to move in. Things couldn't be more perfect for her. She was in a dream world: fucking clueless little bitch, she had to go.

I woke up at sevenish with a thick head. I felt like shit. When I came to, my crap life caved around me all over again. It wasn't a dream, it was a fucking nightmare. *Oh God! She's pregnant!* Her parents were going to go ballistic—and him. They would all kill me, that was a dead cert. The writing was on the wall. What the fuck was going to happen? This baby had to go; it was a fucking mess, complete fucking madness. Abortion was the only option. We needed to sort it quickly, get her to a clinic pronto.

There she was, asleep in my bed with no makeup on. Oh Jesus, that made things even worse, she looked even younger. I lay there, sweatin'. What to do next? She woke up smiling, made me feel even more sick.

"Hey hun, are you OK?" this girl was a total schizo.

"What do you think? No, I'm bloody not. I'm going to get details on-line, to get rid of it. We're too young for this, get it? You'll thank me one day!"

"Don't you want me now I'm pregnant?" She put her arm around me and started to kiss my neck.

"Piss off, Jeanie." I pushed her away. She made me skin crawl. "No, I don't want a bloody baby, not with you or anyone else. I'm too young for this, we hardly know each other. It'll ruin us. You don't get it, do you?"

"Well, I want to have it," she insisted. "You'll come round, once you see it on the scan."

"What the fuck do you think we will live off once your uncle, who already hates me by the way, finds out and sacks me? That's if I'm alive once your dad has beaten me to a pulp. There'll be no scan!" She was clueless.

"They don't care about me. You're the only person who has ever cared for me. Please don't be like this," she pleaded. Then there was sobbing; she was pathetic.

"I'm getting you a cab. You're going home. I'll get info for an abortion."

"What about my parents? Won't they find out?"

"Well, they sure as hell are going to find out soon enough if we do nothing, aren't they, when you start getting big and fat, and you're throwing up every day?" I couldn't even give her eye contact.

I phoned for a cab, got her in it, and sent her on her way.

That morning, Jeanie kept bloody texting me, but I didn't answer all day. She was doing my head in.

    If you don't speak to me by the end
    of the day ul regret it

She kept texting, and because I didn't reply, her texts just got worse. The final text read:

    If you don't answer me, I'm telling
    my parents at 7pm!

I sat there staring at my phone. I didn't know how to handle this girl ... she was a total head case. Just a teenager, for fuck's sake. Jeanie was showing her true colours. And me, I was feeling permanently sick.

    OK, come to mine later

Trying not to lose it, trying to be civil so she didn't do something stupid. It was over: my life, my job, my future, over. All my plans gone.

It was a pretty shit that night for us both. Jeanie kept trying to persuade me that things were going to be OK. I hit the brandy again. She cried, we argued, and that was basically it for the next few days. I needed her to go back home. I mean, at sixteen, did her parents not wonder where she was?

I downloaded a shed load of abortion info off the internet and found a place in Liverpool that would carry out the job. The problem was getting her there. Jeanie was adamant that everything was going her way. According to her vague dates, she thought she was gone about eleven weeks; time was definitely not on our side. We had to get an abortion in the next few weeks otherwise we were stuffed. Meanwhile, I was getting off my face every night and trying my best to hold down my job. I was royally pissed off. Even my staff noticed I was on a downer. I was irritated and snappy. The calm, fun, lovable manager I had been turned into a short-tempered, grumpy git overnight. Shop figures had dropped big time. Will was on my back and loving every minute, wasn't he, seeing me fail at last, the bastard.

Jeanie was hell-bent on having this bloody kid and she was doing my head in. I was going to have to play this very tactfully if it was going to go ahead. I just couldn't help thinking how her parents and Will were going to go ballistic. She had to get rid of it. It was our only way out. Trying to persuade her, however, was another matter. She was a stubborn little bitch.

She was all over me that day. Tryin' to kiss me, but all that did was make me cringe all the more.

"How far gone are you? Are you sure it's only eleven weeks?" I was manic.

"That's no way to greet me, is it?"

I couldn't even look at her; she was making me want to throw up.

83

Two weeks passed and Jeanie was really suffering with morning sickness. She was in a shit mood and foul tempered every day, and she was starting to lay down some rules. Me, I was on the edge with the whole crap situation as madam was dishing out ultimatums. So I dished out my own.

"If you don't get rid of this baby, then we are over and I'm moving abroad!"

She wasn't listening, she just didn't get it, happy in her own bloody world. I had an escape plan—Spain or somewhere like, it was my only sane option. If she didn't get rid of it, then I was going to get on a flight and go live somewhere hot and sunny, anywhere really, I didn't give a shit. This had to be sorted quick, before her parents got wind of it. I bought myself a one-way ticket to Malaga and was going to get some bar job, anything, leave all my shit behind. The flight was booked for the next Saturday night after work. No one would miss me for a couple of days, including her. She had shown her true colours in the last few weeks. It was all set. As soon as I'd booked the ticket, I felt the ton of bricks lifted from my shoulders. The flight was 11.00pm Saturday evening. It was on.

14

Karen

Tuesday 11am

It's another glorious day. Not a cloud in the sky and the heatwave continues. My thoughts turn away from what is happening with Mum and I'm back by your side in intensive care. You're waking for longer periods now, which is great news. but I guess, like us, you're in a lot of shock. You look permanently worried and your eyes are fixed facing the wall now your ranting has stopped. So we just hold hands, and not much is said. I kiss you but there's no eye contact, there's no conversation, nothing. I'm already racked with guilt. I blame myself for the night out, for bidding in the stupid charity do for the weekend away, and you're not helping. Your silent treatment is making me feel even worse. Has the bleed on the brain affected your personality too?

The surgeon arrives bang on time at eleven, accompanied by an ITU nurse.

"Hi Will, I'm your surgeon, Mr. Rivers. How are you doing? How's the pain?"

"I'm in agony, Doc, my leg is killing me." You're perfectly normal with him, you couldn't be nicer.

"OK, we'll keep you on a high dose of pain relief for some time. On a scale of nought to ten?"

"Twelve ... fourteen ..." You squeeze my hand, sweat running from your temples. Even though it's stifling in here, you feel so cold.

He sits next to you. As his eyes meet yours, he clears his throat to speak. "Will, I need to talk to you about your leg."

You try to lift yourself higher in the bed but your wound must have caught on the sheets. Your scream goes right through me.

"It's OK, it's OK, Doc," you reassure us but your face is grey and filmed with sweat. I feel for you.

"When you were shot in your knee, I'm afraid there wasn't a lot for us to repair. Because of the gunshots, an awful lot of tissue, muscle and bone was blasted away. When we operated on you, you also lost a considerable amount of blood. We did all we could to save your leg but I'm afraid we had to amputate from above the knee."

You glance down to the cradle that protects your wound from the bed sheets.

"What? Fuck! No! No!" The tears stream down both our faces. Again, you try to sit upright but the agony jolts you back into the bed. "Ah, shit!" Frantically, you run your fingers through your hair in rage, shock and total disbelief. "But I can feel my leg. You're wrong! I'm in agony here, it's killing me. You can't have taken my leg; I can still feel it. You're wrong, I can feel it!" You are totally out of control, screaming at the surgeon. I have no idea what to do.

"Will, the pain you are experiencing is called phantom pain. Your brain is sending messages to you that your leg is still there. You will have phantom pain for a while, some people maintain feeling in their legs for a couple of months. I'm so sorry, we did all we could. Now we have to concentrate on getting you well, making sure the wound heals, and get you back on your feet with intensive physio and get you fitted for a prosthetic limb."

I can tell you're not taking it in. You won't have it.

"But I can feel my leg," you scream as the nurse rushes to your side to calm you.

The doctor prescribes some more sedation which is injected into the cannula in your hand.

"I'm so deeply sorry," the surgeon says as his parting shot before he and the nurse leave us alone in the room.

You lie there, your face blank, in total silence; I don't know what to say. I hold your hand, my feeble attempt to calm you down. I have no clue what to do. To see you screaming and losing it with the doctor breaks my heart. I've never seen you that way before. Before all this madness happened, you could cope with enormous amounts of stress, running your own business buying and selling expensive cars. It seems disloyal to leave you so I stay by your side whilst you sleep. I'm not exactly sure myself how we are all going to cope. You keep muttering.

"You bastard … I'll find you … you'll pay for this … a fucking gun … my girls … tell her …."

The nurse enters the room discretely. "Do you want me to take you back to the ward, hun? You need to get your rest too. He will be asleep for a few hours now."

I nod and half smile back to her, give you a light kiss on your forehead. It's clammy and you're clearly agitated but the sedation has kicked in and you're fast asleep.

This whole thing is a complete mess. The horror on your face haunts me as I'm taken back to my ward. I'd never seen you break down before. You cried when the twins were born but I'd never seen you lose it like that, not to such an extent. I try to imagine myself in your position. How would I react? It's impossible to say. It is an awful thing to have to hear. Maybe I'd be no different. How am I going to explain this to our girls? Why has all this happened to my happy little family? We have no enemies. Why would

87

someone do this to us? Why, for God's sake, why?

15

Tuesday 2.30pm

The physio tries me on crutches after lunch, just for a few minutes. The blood drains from my face, making me feel faint and light headed, having not stood up for a couple of days. To start with, I am nervous, guarding my foot, petrified of stubbing it against anything solid. It's liberating not to be in a wheelchair though. Then I think of you. How long will you be out of action? How long will you be in a wheelchair? Will you ever be able to walk again? It is all too much for me. My eyes are swollen and tight with tears. *Get a grip, pull yourself together*, I whisper.

I dread having to explain this to the twins. I manage to delay it until the day before they visit you.

"Mummy, when can we see Dad?" they keep asking. "It's been days now."

"Tomorrow might be good, but before you see him, I have to tell you something. Your dad and I are so proud of you both. You both saved his life. When he went to surgery, the doctors tried as hard as they could to fix his leg, but when they put it all back together again there wasn't enough bone and muscle. They couldn't save Daddy's leg and had to amputate it above his knee."

The girls stare, wide-eyed. "What's amp...u...tate mean?"

"What do you mean? Does he not have a leg anymore?"

I swallow hard, look up to the ceiling. I must control these tears. I nod mutely, not trusting myself to speak. They don't understand. Why should they?

"Is it our fault?" Ellie asks, bless her.

"No, sweetheart, without you and Jesse Dad wouldn't be alive. Thank God you two were there."

The girls can't comprehend how their dad is going to live with one leg.

"Will he have to hop?" I knew this wasn't going to be easy, but this brought a smile to my face.

"Yes, Jesse, to start with I suppose he will. In a couple of months, he will wear a false leg.

"I can hop. I could teach him!" Ellie starts jumping around the room. I try to contain a chuckle, then looking at Jesse's sad face pulls me back up.

"Or will he limp like the old man in the supermarket?" Jesse asks earnestly.

"Yes, just like George at the supermarket. Listen, Dad is going to need a lot of help from us. He's going to be very fed up for a while and it's going to take a long time. He might be in hospital for a few months. So what he needs more than anything is our love and to know that we love him more than ever, just the way he is."

However, you on the other hand are still in complete denial about your amputation, which is understandable, it's early days. Together with the events of last Saturday night, it's going to take a long time to become anywhere near normal again. In the afternoon, when you wake, you are again in floods of tears, your face grey and drained and the blank expression remains the same.

"Why has this happened to me?" you keep repeating.

I want to say "to us," as you seem to forget that it's happened to us all. You act as though you were the only one involved in this nightmare. You don't even ask me what happened in the car with this lunatic, it's all about you.

When I explain that the girls are desperate to visit, you refuse point blank to see anyone. I honestly think you'd only have your parents visit if you had the choice, you don't even seem to want to see me anymore. You don't even ask me how I'm doing. It's been a few days now and I don't know how to deal with you. I'm trying to put myself in your shoes but I'm also wondering if your personality change is the result of your head injury. I'm running out of excuses as to how we can delay the girls seeing you. However, I know I have to respect your wishes and so postpone their visit just one more day. Eventually, your parents intervene.

"Come on, son, it'll do you the world of good to see those kids."

You're adamant you don't want to see them, so it takes a lot of persuasion and eventually, "Only a short stay," you insist.

Finally, the day comes. Jesse and Ellie are so excited and, unusually for them, they both wear similar sparkly t-shirts and shorts. I'd forgotten it's still a heatwave outside. In fact, it's so humid I wish it would thunder to clear the air a bit. Everyone is nervous. How is the next hour going to go? What will they say to you? Your mum, bless her, bought some new pyjamas so I help to freshen you up whilst they wait anxiously outside with your parents. When you're ready, I usher them in. They find a gap between the drips on either side of your bed. They cry, you cry, we all cry. The girls try to explain their phone call to the emergency services. Thankfully, they don't mention your leg. You seem to get choked when you speak so you barely say a word. They might only be ten but they're not stupid, so after a while their conversation runs dry and we just sit there in silence.

We stay with you for an hour and when it's time, they don't want to let you go. It's a better tonic than we could have ever imagined. You even have a smile for them. The girls leave and again I am alone with you. You appear to be a bit more lifted. I think it's done you good to see our little ones.

"That went really well," I say whilst rearranging your pillows. "It's going to take time for all of us, Will, we've all been through hell and back." Another one of my attempts to prompt you, to acknowledge that we too were in the attack. "Thank God those two girls were there." Still no reply from you, your eyes fixed to the wall and yet again I'm totally ignored.

I leave you to sleep and the porter wheels me back downstairs; it is too far to come on crutches just yet, though I'm getting better on them.

The rest of my time is spent with Jesse and Ellie. They are subdued; it is a hell of a lot to take in and it's been a very long day. If only I could just reach you, but instead you keep pushing me away. I know you are in a lot of pain and I know you lie on the bed thinking and asking yourself why? Why did this happen to you—but I also hope you ask why it happened to us too? I ask myself the same questions. This evil bastard has changed our lives forever.

16

Jez

Ten years ago

It all went well that Saturday night. I seemed to be on a roll. My staff assumed that I was back to my old self but no sharp knife could cut the atmosphere between me and Jeanie. They knew something was going on, they were a canny lot. They'd all pitched in to tell me to watch my back, warned me that she was a loose cannon. They didn't want me to get into shit with the boss, they were worried I could lose my job. I was taking a massive gamble. The takings that day were the best they'd been in weeks. Everyone that Saturday left the shop on a high. It was all going to plan, but I was shittin' myself. I was never coming back. I felt great. I told Jeanie I wasn't well, that I had a cold coming, that I'd see her on Sunday afternoon, knowing damn well I would be somewhere by the sea in sunny Spain, finding a new job, a new life and a new me.

I practically flew up those stairs to my flat and then stopped dead. There she was, Jeanie. My face must have dropped when I saw her.

"What are you doing here? I told you I wasn't feeling well."

"You don't look ill to me. In fact, you look the best I've seen you for weeks. What's going on?" Her whinging little voice was doing my head in.

"You can't come in." I panicked. If she did she'd see the packed suitcase all ready to go in the lounge, as well as the passport and the one-way ticket to freedom on the kitchen worktop.

"What are you hiding from me, Jez?" This bitch was drivin' me up the wall. "Let me in or I'm going to start shouting."

It was all about to go tits up, but I was adamant that my plan wasn't going to backfire. I still had my ticket. I opened the door and counted to five ... One, Two, Three—

"What's this? You going somewhere? Without me?"

Here we go, it's all going pear-shaped.

"I'm leaving, Jeanie. I've got a plane in three hours and I'm off. I told you we were too young, and you wouldn't have it. I can't stay here. I'm going to lose my job—that's if I don't get murdered first, either by your dad or your tosser of an uncle. I'm finished in England, it's over, we are over. I've tried to tell you to get rid of the baby but you wouldn't have it, would you? We are both too young for this."

The spoilt bitch started to scream. A real mental case. She wouldn't believe what she was hearing; this wasn't in her little plan.

"Jez, no, don't leave me, please. I can't live without you, no one loves me the way you do!" She was off her head.

"Be quiet, keep your voice down, my neighbours will hear you."

"I don't care about your bloody neighbours! I want this baby, your baby. Take me with you, please take me with you." She was well out of order. "Please, Jez." She tried to put her arm around me, but I pushed her back. I wasn't having any of it.

94

"No, it's not happening. What is it with you? You don't listen, do you! How many times have I said it, but it's not going into your head, is it? It was the baby or me, and now I'm off.

She grabbed her phone from her pocket and started to dial.

"Now what are you doing, you silly cow?"

"I'm phoning my mum. I'm telling them everything."

"You're a fucking head case."

"Mum ... Mum ..." She'd got through.

I snatched her phone and threw it across the room, bashing it against the wall.

"Jeanie … Jeanie, love ..." I could hear her mum's voice. "Are you alright? Jeanie, Jeanie?"

I grabbed the phone from the floor and hung up.

"You stupid bitch! What did you do that for?"

"You're not leaving me, Jez!" She was going mental and punched me hard, splitting my top lip.

"Stop it, you fucking nutcase!" I tried to grab her, but she thumped me with her free hand, this time smacking my ear. "You bitch!" I grabbed her wrists, tried to stop her, and pushed her away from me, hard against the wall. There was this god almighty crack. It was her head, she must have whacked it against the coat hook, because she dropped like a stone. I stood over her, horrified. "Jeanie, fuck, I'm sorry, I ... Jeanie, you know I didn't mean it, stop mucking around please. Jesus, I'm so sorry." But she didn't move, she just lay there, staring at me, eyes wide open. Blood poured from the back of her head. It was all so quick. "Oh shit!" What the fuck had I done? I just stood there, staring at her perfect doll face, and a growing pool of dark red blood staining her beautiful blonde hair. I tried to stop the bleeding but instead I was soaked—my hands, my arms, my face—in her blood. Now it really was over, I was finished. I had to think straight. It was an accident, it was self-defence, but how the hell would I explain this and the baby?

I wanted to throw up and just made it to the loo, stuck my head under the cold tap and tried to get a grip. The more I tried to get the blood off me the worse it got. Blood splattered up the bathroom wall as I splashed myself with more and more water. I snatched a t-shirt and downed a massive brandy. I still had that ticket. I'd get on that flight. Grabbing my things, I took one last look at Jeanie, her eyes still open, and fled.

Maybe Jeanie's mum called the police, knowing that something was wrong, I've no idea. To this day, I don't know how they knew my address or where she was. I can only assume they tried to call her back, unless one of the neighbours heard us. I don't know, I'm guessing. Maybe my neighbours had gathered in the corridor to see what was going on, who knows.

Apparently, within the hour the cops were at mine, banging on the door. They knocked the door down and there she was, cold. Jeanie's tiny body slumped on the floor surrounded by a pool of dark blood, her eyes open, her face grey and waxy. Murdered. It must have been obvious to the police that whoever lived in the apartment had left in hurry.

17

Karen

Thursday 11.00am

I am discharged after a few days with an oversized navy blue protective boot and crutches, which are killing my hands but I have to persevere. I suppose my wound is healing as well as could be expected, although it's still agony, especially first thing in the morning.

When your parents bring me home, it is all too much. The house is unbearably quiet and enormous without you. Each room haunts me with our voices from the previous weekend, before we went to that log cabin. We should have just stayed here at home, in our very own paradise—but we didn't though, did we.

The girls are quiet and withdrawn, and your mum has mentioned the nightmares they've been having. They are so different from their usual cheeky selves. Instead they're frightened, inseparable, and subdued. I've left them in front of the TV but they only stare blankly at the screen as cartoons play out before them. It's heartbreaking to see the effect it's had on them. They sit inches apart; nothing is said and yet the sadness in their eyes says it all.

Your dad, desperate for something to do, collects the post from the end of the drive, but when he walks back through the patio door his face is ashen.

"What's happened now?" I can tell something is wrong instantly. Thank God the twins are not in the room.

"I've just found this, love. You'd better sit down for this one."

An envelope with the words 'I KNOW WHERE YOU LIVE. I'M HERE FOR YOU', the letters cut from newspapers, is placed on the kitchen table. I sit hard in the chair. Hairs prickle the back of my neck whilst my blood drains from my face. It's difficult to breathe.

"Oh God, he's insane! What the hell does 'I'm here for you' mean?"

"It's hand delivered, love," your dad says gently, putting his hand on my shoulder. "He's been at the end of the drive!"

I hold my head in my hands and sob.

Your father calls Mike, the inspector in charge of the case. Both he and Tracy, his partner, are at our door within fifteen minutes, followed by forensics. I'm finding it hard to speak.

"Now what … what if he comes here … what if he gets into the house? What'll we do?" I whisper.

"I'll get you a couple of plainclothes officers to stay here over the next few days. Though I don't think he'll come back. He'll know you'll have contacted us, so it's unlikely he'll return. The other officers will be here within the hour. Meanwhile, secure all windows and doors. I'll stay here till they turn up. Try not to worry. That's our job." Mike gives me a reassuring smile.

This guy is so caring, saying all the right things. Except it should be you supporting me, not Mike. As nice as he is, it's you I need right now. I miss you so much.

Forensics dust for prints on the postbox and take the letter away for tests. We sit in complete silence. It is as if the raw wounds of last weekend have opened up all over again. I am a complete wreck.

"What if he's watching us right now? What if he's looking in the window as we speak?"

Mike cups my hands in his. "Karen, listen to me. He's going to make a mistake, it's just a matter of time, and we'll get him when he does."

Your dad tries his best to comfort me whilst I clearly lose it. We never bothered to have curtains at the back of the house because we never felt overlooked. Now I want to board the whole place up until the police finally catch this head case.

Not much is said or done for the rest of the day. The plainclothes police officers arrive after about thirty minutes. They act as if they are old friends of ours at the front door, just in case he's watching.

I'm practically a zombie. I sit with the girls, on guard if you like. We even go to the bathroom together. I don't let them out of my sight.

The twins are oblivious and that's just how I want it to stay. I invent a game that the three of us close all curtains and we check each window and door yet again, over and over; security has become my new obsession.

"Why are these people staying with us?" Jesse whispers.

"Ah, they are police officers, sweetheart, they just need to be here for a few days. Is that OK?"

"OK, Mum."

We hold each other tight. I don't think they'll let me go. It's heaven.

Me and the girls spend the night in our bed, but I don't sleep. I lie there totally terrified. My brain is in overdrive, listening to every single creak, fearing for our lives, with the kitchen knife placed firmly under my pillow. Every time I doze off, a sudden jolt wakes me with a vision of him here in our room: his staring eyes, his foul body odour and the words "I KNOW WHERE YOU LIVE. I'M HERE FOR YOU". The night is still; the only sound is my heart pounding. The girls fidget and they keep waking and shouting, clearly suffering from nightmares. I am completely shattered. Surely we have to try to get some normality. We can't go on like this.

Outside it's still muggy; the heatwave has continued and the rest of the country has enjoyed fantastic weather for this time of year. Normally we would be in the garden barbequing, the girls in the paddling pool, but not now. Things have changed dramatically in the last few days, probably for the rest of our lives. I am overly security conscious, now too scared to even leave a window open, so the house is dry and stuffy. It's stifling, which doesn't help our mood. I am exhausted trying to move around on these crutches and with a lack of sleep and the stress, it's taken its toll. Every time my eyes close, he's there: his eyes, his balaclava, his tongue. I'm petrified.

Each time I visit you've become increasingly withdrawn and nastier towards me. I'm at my wits end. We struggle to talk. The best you can do is "yep", "nope", or "whatever you like". The last time we argued was five years ago, when I reversed your new Jaguar into the tree on the drive, and that was only half a day of silence. I don't know how to deal with your moods, this is alien territory for me. It's obvious you blame me. I blame myself too and I'm desperate for you to be at least pleasant. It's not a good idea to mention the envelope to you either; you have enough on your plate, so for the time being I keep it to myself. I had a chat with your doctor and he suggested a mild anti-depressive.

"It is very common, Karen, for amputees to become depressed. Will's rehabilitation is going to take a few months. Right now, we have to promote his confidence, heal his wound, and get him mobile again."

It's going to be a very rocky road for all of us. We have to pull it together. We need to try to overcome the horrors, to attempt to pick up the pieces, but the nightmares just keep coming. My mind's in overdrive: what if he'd taken the girls, kidnapped us, or murdered you and me, orphaned Ellie and Jesse. I just can't switch it off. The video keeps playing.

Back at home and despite the police presence, I obsessively check doors once, twice, three times. I'm at my wit's end. To think he is out there somewhere observing, watching our girls. What if he were to come back? What if he wants to finish us off, to silence us all for good?

With all the crap that's going on since the letter arrived, I haven't even considered for one minute your job, our finances, your long-term rehab and how we will cope with all this monumental mess. You've always been a very successful, positive man, with your own business, but it relies solely upon you, your personality, and your contacts. You sell very expensive cars to extremely rich clients. It's taken eight years to build your business. What will happen to your PA Julia, and Ralph, your car cleaner? How do we keep them both employed? Ralph's wife has just had a baby, for Christ's sake. You always loved your cars and have become very passionate about work over the years, and business had been excelling. But you need to be at the top of your game and there's no sign of that anytime soon. How are we going to cope? The garage is mortgaged, as is our home, with enough equity in both maybe to purchase a smaller house outright if we need to. Things are going to have to change dramatically. Do we need to sell the house? The problem is it is hard enough to come to terms with our trauma without wondering when you're going back to work.

18

Jez

Ten years ago

Jesus, I never meant to kill her, but now I was stuffed. I got in a cab and headed to the airport, dripping with sweat, my chest like a vice. I struggled to breathe, stuck my head out the window like a family pet all the way to the airport. What the fuck had I done? However annoying she had become in the past few weeks, she didn't deserve this, she didn't deserve to die. I had to get my shit straight, keep it together, get on that plane. It was my only hope. The taxi ride felt like a lifetime, but my flat was only twenty minutes to the airport. I paid the driver—thank god he wasn't a talker. Christ knows what he thought. I stunk his cab out with my sweat, even in the state I was in. The smell was embarrassing.

I was straight in the gents and washed my face and hands, but wasn't enough to stop my sweating. My lip was swollen where Jeanie had thumped me earlier. I soaked some loo roll, put it on my mouth to try to bring the swelling down. As soon as I was dry, more sweat appeared back on my top lip and forehead. It was never ending My t-shirt was dripping, so I took another top from the case and dried the sweat off my body with the old one then threw it in the bin. Practically doused myself in deodorant. *Come on, Jez, get a grip. Deep breaths. Keep cool. One-and-a-half hours to go before takeoff, you're nearly there. OK, mate, let's go. Get some control. Deep breaths.* I kept saying it over an' over.

I wondered what was going on back at my flat. No doubt the police were all over my room by now. I imagined what they were saying. "Check the airports, train stations and harbours. I want this man. I want him arrested. Do we have a recent photo?" Thinking of it, there was only one in the room, not framed. It was a small picture of me and Jeanie, taken eight weeks ago, both looking very happy and very much in love.

I queued at the check-in. It seemed like forever. Images of Jeanie's dead face haunted me. The girl on the desk was checkin' me out. I swear she knew.

"Hello sir. Have you packed the suitcase yourself?" Condescending tart.

"Yes," I managed to get out, my throat raw and dry, my heart beating thick and fast. She could tell, the girl behind the desk could tell, I was convinced. Sweat trickled down my back, my cheeks burned, my top lip sweaty. Jeanie didn't deserve to die. *One more trip to the men's loos after this. Take deep breaths. Come on, Jez, calm down, calm down,* I told myself. *Nearly there.*

I was checked in, grabbed my hand luggage and walked over to X-ray, to departures and, more importantly, the bar. *I can do this. I don't need to go to the loos again. I can do this. Stay calm, Jez,* I chanted over and over. The queue for the X-ray looked a mile long. People all around, buzzing about their holiday. Happy bloody couples, over-excited kids, babies … all I heard was babies crying, happy couples laughing, joking and kissing. It was pissing me off—everyone happy except me. Some three-year-old little shit with clueless parents kept bashing his sit-on carry case into the backs of my legs. I needed that brandy. Now was the time I needed to keep it together. Problem was the more I tried to calm down the worse I got. I had to remove my jacket and belt and place my things into the grey plastic box for the conveyor belt, even remove my shoes. The pale grey t-shirt was now black with sweat; my colour choice couldn't have been worse. To an outsider it was obvious I was nervous about something. The guard behind the conveyor belt glared at me, my dripping t-shirt and my fat swollen lip. *Deep breaths, Jez, we are nearly there.* I sailed through the X-ray machine. I'd made it, thank God. Thank God no more searches. I was through, no man's land departures. Brandy, large one, coming up. Here we go, Jez. My hand luggage, however, didn't. It went behind the glass screen onto the other conveyor belt. Shit. Now I had to join another queue whilst I waited for the guard with his blue plastic gloves to give me the nod.

"Who's is this one?" He pointed to mine and beckoned me over.

My bag was now being searched. Not only that, but another guard was watching me and was now whispering to his colleague. They both stared at me. Did I look suspicious? Of course I did. They bloody knew. Why was this young man sweating so much? What was wrong with his top lip? I knew they knew. Now I had to wait to have my bag searched. I put my jacket back on sharpish, trying to hide the soaking t-shirt, wiped my forehead and stood in the queue, trying my best to control my breathing.

Oh Jesus, they could tell something was up. Why had they singled out my hand luggage? I was so guilt-ridden. It was written all over my face. Jez the cold-blooded murderer. Did I imagine it or had more security guards gathered behind me? My sweating was way out of control.

I knelt down, pretending to tie my shoelace, just to get my breath, get the blood circulating, stop me from passing out, and give myself time to wipe my forehead. A knot developed in my stomach and I was desperate for the loo. Eventually, I dragged my heavy body up and faced a seriously obese, over-zealous head-shaven guard.

"Your bag, sir?" he quizzed.

"Yes." The words barely croaked from my over-dry mouth.

"Don't look so nervous." His gaze was patronising. Wearing his latex gloves, he removed an item slowly from my case. "You should have put this in a plastic bag, mate." He held the deodorant up like some golf trophy, just won.

My chest was tight, a heart attack was imminent. I was convinced I was going down. Sweat trickled down either side of my face, stinging my already burning cheeks. I could feel the presence of someone behind me, either side of me. Collecting my bag, I turned straight into a wall of security guards.

"Do you have a minute? Can we have a word, sir? Would you come this way?"

"Why? I haven't done anything. What's wrong?"

"Just follow us, please sir. This won't take long."

It was over. To be honest, the relief was huge. My ears pulsed, my heart throbbed through my soaked t-shirt, my stomach bubbled. I felt sick with terror. They'd got me. I was going down for this, down for a very long time: prison, murder, life. Oh God! I threw up.

19

Karen

Thursday 4.45pm

Back home, Mike, now practically our resident plainclothes policeman, is here to restore my new iPhone with its previous data from my laptop. Mike has become one of the family. I've seen him every day since the attack, and he's taken on your role. He's the one who makes me feel safe and protected. He's caring, sympathetic and considerate—all the things you're not at the moment, but I'm still hopeful that thing will improve as time moves on. We sit there and wait. Once fully downloaded, the familiar sound comes as a text arrives, exactly what they are hoping for. The beeping continues as text upon text loads onto my phone.

Louise:
How are you hun?

Text number one.

Zane, my hairdresser:
Thursday's appointment

```
confirmation
for 2.45pm.
```

Text number two.

Number three was a close-up image of one piercing blue eye and the words:

```
I've got my eye on you.
```

The blood drains from my face and I feel a lurch in my stomach. The back of my eyes sting as I'm determined to hold back more tears. Your mum grabs my hand tight in hers.

Text number four:

```
I've seen you naked. You're so hot
```

"Oh my God. What does he want?"
They crowd around me, your dad's hands firmly on my shoulders, your mum continues to hold my hand.

Text number five is Louise again:

```
Worried about you hun.
Can you ring me.x
```

Text number six:

```
Loved you in that red dress.
```

"How does he know about my red dress? I had no clothes on when he—" I stop abruptly as my face colours at the memory that this madman has seen me naked and everyone in the room knows it. I breathe in deeply and continue, "I've only ever worn it once. I didn't have it with me in the cabin. Why won't he just go away, why won't he just leave us alone?"

"We need to step up security. For the moment, we are unable to trace his phone, but we have had some new developments." Mike radios HQ to get more officers.

Text number seven:

LET'S GET RID OF HIM, KAREN

Number eight:

WHY DID YOU MARRY THAT
TOTAL PRICK? IT SHOULD
HAVE BEEN ME.

Number nine:

I WASN'T SUPPOSED TO SHOOT YOU,
BUT I HOPE HIS LEG HURTS.

"I have an officer at the hospital and he will remain outside his room for as long as it takes. Think, Karen, is there anyone with a grudge against you or Will? Anyone with a crush on you? Ex-boyfriend? Work colleague?"

I take a deep breath, staring at the wall as my eyes glaze over. What could we do? What could anybody do but wait? The police assign a further two unmarked police cars to patrol around the village, but they're nowhere nearer to catching this psycho.

Your dad sets about organising a security response company linked to the alarm, so should the alarm go off, they would be there within four minutes with a guard dog in tow. The alarm guys will fit the house with hidden panic buttons. The gates—for the time being, even if they are just wooden hand-operated gates—will make me feel a bit more at ease. Your dad has purchased copious amounts of barbed wire from the local farm shop, and our gardener is here this afternoon to assemble it around the perimeter fence. Our home is going to be a fortress.

"We are going to attempt to trace the sender so we need to take your phone to the station. I've got some questions for you. When did you last wear the red dress?"

"I don't know … it's brand new. I've only worn it once … Christmas, Christmas at the Midland Hotel, Manchester."

"Can you remember the date?" He scribbled down some notes.

"Um, God, yes, it was a cancer charity dinner, Friday night, the last Friday night before Christmas, whenever that was."

"Was there anyone there acting odd?"

"No, I don't know, we had a great time. Shit, it was just a typical charity do." I rack my brains trying to recall that night, but it was five months ago. *Think Karen, think* I say to myself.

"Can you remember anything?"

"Yes, of course, that's where I bid for the log cabin, but there was no one there that knew us, other than the people on our table. I didn't recognise anyone. All the people on that table were our friends. None of them would do this to us."

Mike looks at his colleague who was standing by the door and gives him a quick nod. The officer leaves the room, presumably to follow this up.

"I'm going to need a list of everyone you knew at that event, including the people on your table," Mike says firmly.

"But–" I try to interrupt.

"Karen, we have to consider every eventuality. Did Will speak to anyone apart from the people on your table?"

"I don't know, we were drinking champagne all night, and we had to leave the table for more drinks or …"

"Did either you or Will upset anyone that night,"

"No, I don't think so, no."

"Were you together all night, you and Will? Could Will have upset anyone?""

"No, he's not like that. He only left me when he went to the bar or the loo or to go outside for a cigar a couple of times. He wouldn't upset anyone. He's kind and gentle. It's not his style."

"OK, Karen, great, that's brilliant. We'll get on to The Midland and see who was working in the room that night and see if there's maybe any CCTV."

Feeling safer with officers downstairs, I insist the girls sleep in their own room although they kick up a fuss. I boil the kettle, make myself some chamomile tea, two teabags—I am determined to get some sleep—take a couple of pain killers, and go to bed. We all have to try to get some normality back as soon as, despite my fears. I know it sounds cruel, but allowing the girls to sleep in our bed every night will just make them worse. It's short lived though, because at 3am two glorious little bodies creep in either side of me. It's such a comfort. I have to admit I can sleep better with them by my side.

20

Jez

November 6 months ago

I'd got myself a decent little waiter's job at the Midland
Hotel. Lied through my teeth on my C.V. and managed to
fudge around those few years at Her Majesty's pleasure—
no one checks them anyway, do they? I'd been there for a
couple of weeks. It looked like my life was back on track.
That was until the night of the Christmas do, when I saw
both of them together again. They looked rich, happy and
totally carefree. I was fucking fuming. Neither of them
had changed; he still had that stuck up, arrogant prick look
about him; she still looked fit and gorgeous, she hadn't
aged an inch. Me, I was unrecognisable. I'd not had a
carefree ten years, had I? I'd done time. I did have a laugh,
though. I served them both that night; they had no clue
who the fuck I was—hilarious.

When the bids began, he was straight in there, the big
I am—what a tosser! Made me want to punch his lights
out. He acted like he was loaded. What a complete dick!
I managed to stay in the ballroom the whole night whilst

that auction was on.

Except when I had my break and was allowed outside for ten minutes and so I went for a fag. Guess who was there. I'm sure he recognised me, he kind of did a double take, especially when I spoke to him when I offered him a light. I knew it was risky but it was too good an opportunity to miss. I had a great laugh about it for days after that.

Maybe I'd find out their home address, but I didn't need to, did I? Towards the end of the auction she bid for the log cabin. That log cabin was a specific weekend in May, the address was on the auction list. I could have a bit of fun with them, make them both freak out for a few hours, be frightened for the night, just like I had been for my last ten years. Definitely the best night I'd had for a long time.

Bingo, his missus won the bid. It was fate. I couldn't believe my fucking luck. I'd dreamt about this when I was inside, never thought it would happen though. Funny how shit happens and gems like these fall on you lap sometimes. My luck was changing. Now it was my chance to get some payback. It had turned out to be a brilliant night

Afterwards, back in my shitty halfway house, I poured a huge brandy and congratulated myself. For the first time in ten years I was a very happy man indeed. I was going to have to meticulously plan this attack. I had all the time in the world, five long months in fact. I couldn't wait to see them both again, especially her. Burglary should do it. I didn't need to *harm* them; I just want to see them shit themselves for a few hours.

Prison time had its bonuses. I did time with some seriously nasty blokes, proper professional bastards. I'd mastered the art of drug taking, learnt how to take care of myself and look out for number one. My cellmate had passed on a few of his skills, he was a clever bloke. He was inside for phone and computer hacking so you could say he was my go-to man when in I needed a bit of IT support. We were both released within weeks of each other so I'd purchased my dodgy little mobile from him, one that couldn't be traced of course. When April came round, I bought a gun from one of my ex-cellmates. He was released three months before me, a real hard case. Shaved shiny head, tattooed face, he sure frightened the crap out of me. I wasn't going to use it properly, you understand, I just wanted to frighten the shit out of them both, maybe get some money. It was all about a bit of payback. I couldn't wait; May was coming around nicely.

That weekend, I'd got a train to Crewe, then on a bus to the nearest village to the log cabin. I'd got there about three-ish, my rucksack full of brandy and dope, a few packs of sandwiches to keep me going and binoculars from the Army and Navy. I was a good distance from the cabins but near enough to see what was going on. The kids were a bonus I'd not planned for—bargaining chips. I kept an eye on them all afternoon, with the lovely Karen looking so hot. They were all so cosy, a real happy little family. That pissed me off even more. I watched them laugh and joke. He wouldn't keep his hands off her—it made me want to throw up. The little girls in the hot tub, the smug fucking parents knocking back the wine, this pathetic little happy family. *I'll get you when you're asleep.* I couldn't wait. Bring it on, Jez. I was on top form. I couldn't have planned it better if I tried.

When they left for their little bike ride, it was the perfect time to get a bit closer. I had a snoop around, checked it out. It gave me more of an idea of the layout. I had to get a plan, get it straight in my head. I had to get my shit together. It was time to go back into the woods, rest, eat and wait.

Time was ticking. I was bored, and I was itching to get on with the job. They took forever to go to bed. I nodded off and woke up about 2.30. A bit of Dutch courage needed.

Lit myself a spliff and tried to calm my nerves. I was still a bit twitchy so I threw down the rest of the brandy. That did the job and I was ready for the kill—not literally, you understand. Couldn't wait to see their faces, especially him. I wanted him to really shit himself. This was going to be a right crack up. I circled the cabin to find the best way in— the open balcony door to their bedroom. *So, you little tosser, did you leave a door open for me, Will? Sloppy! You just never know who, or what, is prowling around outside, do you?*

He was snoring. I could hear it all the way outside. It cracked me up even more. It was a cloudy, humid night. I could have done with a bit of moonlight but instead it was pitch black, no light pollution, not out here, not in the middle of nowhere. I nearly fell over a small table outside. A slight breeze was billowing the curtain beyond the door. I'd never done a burglary before, so I was pretty worked up myself. *Come on, mate.* I gave myself a bit of a pep talk and stood outside the door trying to get my act together. My hands were shakin'. I took a deep breath and crept in. A shaft of light shone onto the dressing table but to get to it I had to negotiate all the crap on the floor: shoes, lace knickers, her clothes. Christ, I thought I was untidy! I could just make out a table to the left with a massive lamp on top. I was sweatin' like a pig. What if it all went wrong? I knew she had some expensive jewellery but I couldn't see it anywhere. I sneaked my way in carefully, had a little shuffle around. When I was in, I wanted to make a bit of noise. I needed them both to wake up, shit themselves when they saw me, me and my balaclava. So, I kicked over the suitcase. I wanted them to taste a bit of fear, the fear I'd had every single day and night for the past ten fucking years. *Bingo—lights, and action.* Here we go! Oh my God, it was so hilarious. He was all cowered in his bed, with the very gorgeous Karen by his side. I had to congratulate myself that in fact they were both shitting themselves. Not so smug now, was he, with my gun pointed straight

114

towards his head.

"If you make a fucking sound I will kill you, your wife and your two brat kids." I spat the words at them. I felt powerful. This was a major turn on.

Grabbing a very fit Karen by the arm, I dragged her into the kitchen. She was a little cracker. The tart didn't wear any pj's either—she hadn't gone down the mumsy route, she was stark naked. What a body! I almost forgot what I was there for. She was a serious distraction and in bloody brilliant shape, with two kids as well, everything exactly where it should have been, just how I like my women. She made me excited—that was definitely not what I'd planned for.

OK, keep your cool mate, you don't want to blow it now. She still looked good enough to eat. I hadn't seen a woman like that in ten very long years. "Where's your fucking money, jewellery, cards, car keys, bitch? You're going to pay!" Wow, she was sweatin' and her skin turned bright red. Sweat was trickling down her cleavage. Was she getting a kick out of this too? I couldn't keep my eyes off her. I wondered if I turned her on. I bet she'd like me without my mask, I bet she'd like a bit of rough. "I want money. Get your coat. You're going to pay me back. We're going for a little drive now, rich bitch. Move or you all die... get it?"

She threw her jewellery on the table and snatched at the nearest coat; it was his, I think. He was pretty gutless. Really surprised me. Not the big 'I am' I'd expected. I mean, where was the tough guy now, eh? He wasn't helping the missus, that's for sure! I planned to sort him out when I got back, back from quality time with Karen, just to make him shit himself a bit more.

He came out of nowhere, the tosser, as bold as brass, and tried to jump me but I was way too quick for him. All those workouts inside paid off. "Shit!" I panicked—three gunshots. He was on the floor. "Shit ... Shit ... Shit." That sobered me up. I wasn't supposed to shoot. What the fuck had I done? I wasn't going back down. Thinking on my feet, I grabbed her jewellery, pushed her out and into the car. I never meant to shoot, fuck, just frighten them both. It was supposed to be a robbery. My head was all over the place. *Now what?* I wasn't going back inside. *OK, Jez, think man, think. Get a grip of yourself.*

The roads seemed endless. Where was the fucking nearest village? On and on, one lane after another. Where the fuck were we? Where was she goin'? Did they not believe in signposts here? *Come on, Jez, think. You need to get this bitch out of the car. Just take the car, take the car, mate.* Finally, a small village, a cashpoint. Jesus Christ, at last.

"Stop the car, there's a cashpoint right here, move!"

She was so bloody slow. She was shakin' like crazy, but I couldn't help but feel for her. I didn't want to hurt her, she was so helpless, made her even more sexy. I just had to kiss her, touch her. This was too good a thing to miss. I tried before I threw her out towards the cashpoint but she turned her head away and rejected me. She was better than me, wasn't she! Not rich enough for her, was I? Stuck up bitch, or was she playin' hard to get? Was she messing with my head?

"Get out of the car. Get me some cash, you bitch, move it!"

She lost it big time but I just shoved her towards the cashpoint. Her shaking hands handed me the money. She was lookin' pretty terrified and I was getting hornier by the minute. Half of me wanted to hold her tight but I had a job to do.

"That's all I can get out a day, £750."

What? All this shit for £750? That wasn't the deal. I snatched the cards from her. "Don't waste any more of my time. What's the fucking number, you stupid cow?" I screamed, my face pushed hard up against hers.

"3750…"

I had to get rid of her. I couldn't go back now I'd shot

him, so I blasted one little bullet at her foot. Not so bad, just a flesh wound. I jumped back in the car and sped off. Now I was shittin' myself. Where the fuck was I? I had to get rid of that car pretty quick or the cops would have me. *Come on, Jez, think.* Where was I? At last, a dual carriageway, a signpost, Crewe 7 miles. I didn't know the area. A train station, thank fuck. *OK, dump the car, get to the station. Keep calm, Jez, keep calm. You're not going down again. Keep your cool, man.*

21

Karen

Friday 10.15am

Home security was all I could think about. Writing endless lists, even my lists had lists. Home just wasn't feeling safe anymore. Will I ever be relaxed again? Every hour I'd check windows, doors, made sure they were locked, reinforced the message to the twins and your parents, my obsession.

The nightmares are persistent, my sleep pattern two to three hours per night. I am shattered. When I last spoke to the police, they gave me a few hints.

"Better gates at the front of the house would be good deterrent, alarm inside the house. But if a burglar wants to get in, they will stop at nothing. Your house looks like a great place to loot. Sorry to be blunt, but your posh cars outside are an attraction, get them in the garage. If you get a security company linked to your alarm, that would be a good idea."

"My father-in-law has already arranged that."

"Great. A sign maybe saying the name of the security company, CCTV in operation, and another sign, 'beware of the dogs' will also help."

"We've put barbed wire up. Is that OK? I know it's not usually allowed, but I don't care. I just want to be safe."

"You can use barbed wire if it makes you feel better. When you get a security company, get them to put a sign outside your driveway that would deter intruders and make them go elsewhere. Get a dog. I suggest a bloody great big one."

At last, Mum is now in the NHS system and has constant care. It's a relief that she is being seen to, but in the last few weeks her Alzheimer's has escalated. The social worker rings me to arrange the next stage of action. We agree to meet tomorrow. With everything else going on, I could do without it, but this needs to be sorted and it is unsafe for her to be on her own.

All five of us visit you for the afternoon, accompanied by the plain clothes policewoman. I'm beginning to dread my time with you but for the sake of the girls I force myself to be upbeat in the hope that by some miracle your indifferent moods towards me might change. However, as usual you're lovely to everyone else. I'm ignored again but I'm getting used to this treatment. I know you blame me for this whole thing. The more I think about it I do believe this is now a character change due to your brain injury. There's no eye contact and any form of affection went ages ago. You keep going on about my jewellery and insurance claims, as if you think that's all I'm worried about. No amount of money will ever bring our sanity back, or your leg. You do try to make a small effort with our girls but nothing with me. It's embarrassing as I know your parents see it too. I speak to one of the staff nurses to ask her opinion. Like me, she too agrees it could be a result of your brain injury. All I want is for it all to go back, back to how we used to be. Instead my heart is breaking and slowly I'm losing my soulmate.

"Karen, he's so down. This could delay his recovery. His wound is healing well, but mentally it's looking like he hasn't accepted it—some people don't. Is there anything else he's worried about? I know it's early days, but he needs anti-depressants and counselling. He's refusing all help on that score. With the flashbacks and nightmares, he only sleeps for a couple of hours, which will add to his anxiety."

"I don't know what to do. He's totally alienated me, it's like I don't exist. Please just give him the antidepressants and don't tell him. We'll have to deal with every day as it comes. He has to pick up. I can't do this without him."

The following day I attend the meeting arranged by a lady from Social Services. Her name is Jenny Crawford. She's plump, at least six inches shorter than me with the shiniest dark brown hair I've ever seen. A neat bob haircut frames the prettiest face with enormous blue eyes. She seems to love what she does as her smile never leaves her face. I'm instantly drawn to her warm and caring personality. The police had already filled Jenny in with our current situation and she is very sympathetic.

"We've been assessing your mum for a while. It's become increasingly obvious that she needs specialist care now. I know you have been up against it. However, your mum's neighbours mentioned she was wandering along the high street in the early hours of the morning, wearing just her dressing gown. I visited yesterday and Mary had left the gas on. The whole place could have gone up. Now, due to your circumstances in the last few weeks, it's impossible for you to be there for your mum and your family. I have had notice today of a vacancy in a residential home two miles from your home. We could try her in there for a two-week period, even if just to give you a break. What do you think?"

This is all too much for me. Things are happening far

too quickly and I have a sinking feeling that now she's under social services supervision everything is becoming way out of my control. Is this really happening? My entire life seems to be going rapidly in a downhill spiral.

"OK," I manage to whisper. "Just a trial. Promise me if it doesn't work out she can go back to her own home."

"I can promise you, but you must agree that since she was hospitalised, her confusion has escalated. Once she has settled in, you will have quality time with her. Professionals can do the caring for her and you can spend the rest of your mum's days enjoying her company."

The words "rest of her days" broke my heart. Nails were already being placed firmly on the coffin, and I held the hammer in my hands. I'm very much alone here with zero support from you, and some lunatic criminal is invading our lives. It is sending me way over the edge.

"We can get the ball rolling and try her out on Monday, if you like; it's a wonderful place, fantastic staff with a great reputation. I know your feelings about her going into a home, and if I wasn't sure of this place I honestly wouldn't suggest it. Do you want to come with me now and go see it, meet the staff? They won't be expecting us. It's the best time to see it, the staff won't be prepared. Do you have the time right now?"

"OK." I feel like I'd been hit by a freight train and it was whisking me away at high speed.

Your dad accompanies me and the social worker to visit the home. It is just as Jenny had described, a beautiful Edwardian house, with 27 bedrooms in various extensions. In the lounge there's a small incubator with tiny chicks that has the attention of a few older ladies. A bingo session is going on in the enormous day room and most of the residents have gathered there to play. One of the ladies shouts "House!" and they all cheer for Doris, a petite lady who can only be about four foot, who has won. She's immaculately dressed in a pink floral dress and is beaming from ear to ear. They whistle and clap as she says she has never won a single thing in her life before. Going into the dining room, it's all laid out beautifully, like an expensive restaurant with crisp white tablecloths, fresh flowers and burgundy napkins to match the patterned wallpaper. They are preparing afternoon tea and cakes for the residents, and the baking smells delicious. Proudly on the wall hang several 'Best Homes in Cheshire' awards. We meet some of the staff, who are incredibly warm and welcoming, and the majority of the residents seem really happy—that for me is the main thing. One little lady is a bit confused. She reminds me of Mum, only about ten years older; same height, same good posture. The amazing thing is she looks so well kept: her hair looks fresh from the hairdressers, she's smart and even has had a manicure by the look of it. Unlike Mum, who is in dire need of a makeover and has in recent years refused point blank to have a haircut. She is being helped back into the conservatory, where another group of ladies are watching *Singing in the Rain* on a huge screen, singing along to the songs they know, accompanied by a few of the staff. Our favourite film when I was younger, we'd watch it every year without fail.

"Come on, let me show you the holiday room for your mum."

Jenny takes us towards the rear of the home, an area designed for dementia and Alzheimer's patients. It's an adorable little room with magnolia walls, a large navy blue floral bedspread with matching curtains, a good sized en-suite bathroom fitted with all the safety gadgets Mum now needs, including a sit-in shower, an emergency red buzzer cord dangling from the ceiling. The bedroom houses a large oak wardrobe with dressing table and mirror, next to a small single bed. It is pretty basic. Jenny suggests I bring Mum's favourite chair and decorate the room with photographs to stimulate her memory and make it a bit more homely.

Through the window is an adorable garden with a stunning view of the Cheshire plains: cobalt wooden benches, tables and chairs are dotted here and there offering a quiet haven for residents and families to enjoy a bit of fresh air. The majority is paved for easy wheelchair access. Borders are lined with curves of lavender from which I can almost taste the delicious fragrance through the open window; a variety of terracotta pots hold exquisite arrangements of purple- and yellow-tipped pansies dancing in the gentle breeze, giving it that French Mediterranean feel. Boxed in wooden sleepers is a small selection of fresh herbs.

"The colours and smells are there to stimulate the residents," Jenny explains.

"It's beautiful! I can see Mum out there, she always loved to potter in the garden."

"This garden is like something from a magazine," your dad exclaims with envy. "They must have a dedicated gardener."

"No, they don't at all. They have a weekly group called the Garden Club. It's basically great therapy for some of the old folk. The staff work together with some of the more able residents, and they maintain it between them. It is a fabulous home. There are loads of activities for the old folk here. A bus takes them all out to the village every Friday and to the local garden centre Tuesday mornings. They are well looked after. My own grandmother was here until June last year, when she passed away."

"Tell you what, love, when our time comes, can you book me and the wife in here too? I think it's a cracking little place," your dad says with a wink. He's so sweet. He can tell by my face how guilt-ridden I feel.

After the viewing, we talk about all the legalities if she were to stay after the trial period. Mum would have to sell her apartment, of course, and a monthly payment would be put in place.

"Do you want to bring her this Monday? It's just I need to know. I've put you at the top of the list because of your situation, so if you can let me know ASAP."

"Trial?"

"Yep, it's a trial."

"OK, let's do it." I take a deep breath and try to control my own feelings. This is not about me anymore, it's Mum who needs the help.

"Karen, your mum will be like her old self, you'll see. Once the carers start feeding her regular meals again, and she receives proper medication. The day spa ladies will go to work on her hair and nails, she'll be transformed. Trust me."

"I do trust you," I say with a weak smile. "We'll drop her off on Monday, but then I will come back in the afternoon, when she can't see me, to drop off her clothes and toiletries. I don't want her to remember that I brought her here."

Your dad and I don't say a word to each other on the way back to the house. When we arrive, there are more developments from my mobile.

"We have more texts; we suspect you may know this guy." Mike puts a reassuring hand on my shoulder. He looks desperately sorry for me, which upsets me all the more. It should be you comforting me, not someone I've only known for a short time.

Text 1:
DIDN'T SET OUT TO HURT YOU KAREN.

Text 2:
PLEASE FORGIVE ME. I'M SO SORRY.

"He's remorseful. I don't think he wants to harm you."

As much as Mike is trying to play it down, it's making me question what this weirdo wants. Why won't he just leave me alone? The sooner he's caught the better.

The weekend is horrendous: the girls are clingy and upset, and with no car to drive I am going stir crazy. You are an empty shell and you're horrible to me yet again; our relationship is spiralling rapidly out of control. I know you blame me. Christ knows I blame myself too. None of us would be in this mess if we'd just stayed in that Friday night. All I want is our lives back to the way it was, a bit of normality. I just want to jump in the car with you, Ellie and Jesse and get away as far as we possibly can. As amazing as your parents are, I need time with you and the girls, to grieve. I feel like someone has died. I'm a prisoner in my own home, and now I'm being stalked by some complete lunatic and he's out there, watching.

Then there is Mum. How is this all going to work out? I've concocted an idea that I will tell her I am taking her to the doctors to get her out of the house. Cruelly, with her diseased brain, by the time we get to the residential home, I figure Mum will have forgotten where she was going in the first place.

Monday is here quicker than I'd hoped. Off we go on the now familiar journey to Mum's apartment, with an unmarked car closely behind us. Bless her heart, she's all ready for me after my phone call instructing her to get ready for the surgery. She's made an effort because she is going to see the doctor, even her hair is brushed. Fighting back the tears is the most difficult thing. This is the greatest act of deception I have ever done in my life, betraying my own mother.

"Hi Mum, how are you doing? Are you nearly ready?"

I look around the room, remembering all the times we've had there: me, Mum and Dad. This could be our very last few moments in this apartment together, sadly, if all goes to plan. Though it is the last thing I want. Going into a home is another step towards death in my opinion.

How I manage to hold it together for the next hour or so, I don't know, but I have to. Mum is so sweet, confused but so sweet. She looks so small and so smart, all dressed up with her best coat on, not knowing what her double-crossing daughter is about to do. I lean against the window with the back of my hand over my mouth, desperate to keep my tears at bay. If I cry she will know something's up, she knows me too well. There's a low eerie mist outside; no doubt the sun will burn through it later but for the moment it suits my mood. We drive with your dad, and not much is said until we reach the home. He stays in the car park whilst the inevitable happens.

"Why are we here? This is not the Doctor's," Mum asks. "Look at all those old people asleep in the day room," she remarks, her eyes as sharp as ever.

I walk behind her and the staff make a bee line for us.

"Hello Mary. Let's take your coat, darling. Come in and have nice cup of tea and cake with us."

"Oh that's very kind of you, how sweet. Thank you, that'll be lovely. Who are you? Are you the doctor?"

I have made eye contact with the head carer, Lisa, my eyes and nose stinging with tears. I can't speak or even say goodbye. The carer nods then ushers her away into the dining room. I leave, walking fast so no one will see my red face and streaming tears. I run into your dad's arms. This is one of those times when I really need you. I love your dad, he's amazing and he holds me tight, rocks me like a baby. But he's not you. I can't speak. Even though she will be only two miles away, the deceitful act I have just done to my own mother, my own flesh and blood, the ultimate betrayal, fills me with guilt which paralyses me. I feel like Mum has just died and I've stuck the knife in. We drive home in silence.

"How's Nanny?" ask the girls, but the lump in my throat is so enormous I cannot speak. Instead, I just nod my head, flee upstairs and pour my heart out. I don't want the girls to see me this way. It seems like the events in last few weeks have all at once hit home.

Lisa phones me later in the afternoon to reassure me that Mum is having a smashing time and has no idea how she got there. I explain that I'm too upset to go back there that afternoon with her clothes, I'll bring them tomorrow when I visit. She convinces me that Mum is in good hands and not to worry.

The rest of the day is a quiet one. That's why your parents have visited you on their own. I needed your support today. I couldn't face yet another day of rejection with you, so I stay at home, put *Snow White and the Seven Dwarfs* on the telly, eat chocolate, drink wine and cuddle with our girls: a warm cosy end to a hateful day. The officers keep their distance in the kitchen area, planning their next move.

It's Tuesday morning and it's a glorious day. I've plucked up enough courage to go to the home to face my mum. I'm expecting tears—from her or from me, I'm not sure. I hand over her suitcase to a member of staff and we sit in the family room, drinking tea, giving details of her life: her likes, dislikes, what she eats, things she used to do.

"Well, she seems to have settled really well so far. We have told her she is only here for two weeks' holiday, and she's OK with that. She has such wicked sense of humour, we've all been in stitches today. Mary has been sat outside our offices giving all the staff jip. We think she's a great laugh. She won't go into the dayroom yet, though," Lisa reports, a kind smile trying to reassure me. "'I'm not sitting in there with all those old fogeys,' she says. Bless her, she's such a character."

"That's a relief. I've been too scared to come over."

"That's normal, my love. Go see her, she looks fab. She's had quite a bit of pampering this morning."

I thought Mum was going to go ballistic and scream at me for betraying her, for doing the one thing she asked me not to do when she was younger. "Don't ever put me in a nursing home." Instead, I am taken aback by the smart little lady in front of me. I am determined not to cry, so I take a deep breath. *Control yourself*, I say to myself. What an instant transformation! Her hair has been expertly quaffed by a professional hairdresser, her nails manicured and polished with deep pink varnish. She looks just like the smart mum who had gradually disappeared over the past two years.

"Mum, you look lovely, really lovely."

"I'm on holiday here for two weeks. The ladies here are super." She gestures towards a plaque on the wall which says 'Mary's holiday home. Here for 2 weeks'. It has been placed there as a reminder, to stop her being even more confused. "I'm sure me and your dad stayed here years ago, when you were a teenager. Just love Cornwall, don't you? The food is wonderful, darling. You must stay for lunch. Are you stopping here the night?"

So there it is, Mum is convinced she is on holiday in a lovely B&B in Cornwall. That's a result I hadn't expected.

"Darling, why are you in that large boot and crutches?"

"I told you, Mum, I fell off my bike and broke a bone in my foot."

"Oh, you know me, you know how shocking my memory is. I can't remember what I did this morning," she laughs "How are Will and the girls?"

"They're good. They will come to see you next time I'm over."

"That's nice."

I stay and chat. It is the same conversation every two minutes, the conversation that I have got used to hearing over the past years thanks to her Alzheimer's, but I don't mind.

"So, how are you? How's Will? How are the girls doing? I forget their names. How's Will's parents?" Over and over. I've learned how to respond to her, not to get angry. It isn't her fault; her brain is diseased. I always answer the question, sometimes different answers just to stop the monotony, to spare my sanity, but I've learnt never to become angry. Dad and I had shouted a couple of times at Mum back in the early days, saying "Yes, you've just said that," or "Mum, stop repeating yourself," or "Stop being so dopey," totally unaware that there was a serious underlying problem going on, and not knowing how to cope with it. Getting annoyed wasn't the answer. Seven years down the line and now with a true diagnosis, I know how to deal with Mum without both of us getting upset. Time with her is a real joy. I'd never thought I'd get this again in her lifetime; it's a long time coming. You'd been right all along, Will; a home was definitely the answer.

After an hour, it is time to visit you. I have to admit I'm reluctant. I don't want to leave her but I'm desperate to see you to tell you the good news that you were right and that Mum looks amazing in the care home. I kiss Mum's soft cheek and say my goodbyes. Jenny, the social worker, has been worth her weight in gold. Mum looks like her old self again, possibly even ten years younger. For the first time in three years, visiting her has been an absolute pleasure. We spoke about the old days when Dad was around and laughed at how daft he always was. It's Mum's short term memory that has gone, she can remember vividly all the things that have happened in the past.

"So, how was she?" your dad asks when I'm back at the house.

"Amazing, really amazing. I loved seeing her: no cleaning, no washing, no shopping, no stress, just quality time. Her hair has been washed and set, her clothes were cleaned and ironed, her nails had been manicured and she smelled like my mum again. They even sprayed her with my perfume, the Chanel no 5 I bought her for Christmas. It's the best thing that's happened to me in weeks. I could kiss that social worker."

22

Jez

Sunday Bank Holiday morning 11am

Some addict was bangin' on my door outside, rambling an' talking shit.

"Piss off!" I shouted. It was the third time that week he'd woke me up. A few minutes kicked in before I remembered the past night. What the fuck had I done? I had to get out of there. I hated it there anyway, that place was worse than my cell. It was a proper shithole. My mattress had been through a few hundred people judging by the stains all over it. There was nothing on the windows to stop the light getting in, not that you could see through the filthy glass anyway. When I first got there I had three coat hangers and a broken old rail—still I had no clothes to put on it. The lamp on the table looked like a death trap—loose wires all over the place, plus it didn't work. The whole place stunk of piss an' I reckon there was more drugs and addicts knockin' around there than there was in Strangeways. People stoned, hangin' around in doorways, tryin' to get in your room. I felt safer inside. In fact, for the first week I barricaded myself in there at night time. I couldn't stay there. Anyway, I had no intention to. I needed to grab my stuff and get out. I didn't have much anyway, I'd not accumulated anything in the six months I'd been there, I couldn't afford it. I had to get the fuck out of there, fast.

My head was banging. I was groggy, my mouth like sandpaper. I had the major hangover from hell, made worse by the aftereffects of a shed load of weed. And I stank. What the fuck had I done this time? Yes, I wanted to scare the shit out of them both, but I didn't need to shoot. I was only supposed to rob them. What possessed me to take a loaded gun? What the fuck was I thinking? I needed to think, and fast. Where had I gone from the village to the train? Where had I left the car? I had been so smashed I hadn't worn gloves, so the cops could be round pretty fast. Did anybody see me? Christ, I'd been hammered. It was hard to piece everything together. Where would CCTV be? Would it all be on the news or in the papers? I didn't have a telly. I needed to check out the newspapers at the shop. Would I be recognised? How much time did I have? I needed to get my shit together, and sharpish. I still had her cards. I thought I could probably use them one more time before they were traced, then sell them on. I had a few hundred quid of their cash, of course.

I boiled the kettle, made myself a strong coffee, then grabbed a bag and filled it with anything I could. I had to get out of the city for good. I kept getting flashbacks of the night before, playing then rewinding, and playing, messing with my head. I couldn't switch off the image of Karen. Christ, she'd looked better than ever. I had her on replay in my head and I was happy she was there. I wanted to see her again, but how was that going to work?

I almost forgot I had her mobile, didn't I. Switched it on and there was a sickly family pic of the four of them, all lookin' happy. Made me want to throw up. No passwords required—sloppy Karen, very sloppy—so I swiped to the photos. I couldn't resist lookin' at shots of them both, scrolled the pictures back to December to see her in that dress. Christ, she looked good. She reminded me a bit of Jeanie at our works do in that red dress. The phone gave me everything—inside knowledge of where they'd all holidayed in the past three years, her bank details but, more importantly, thanks to WhatsApp, I had their home address. I'd found some top info—thank you—that could lead me straight back to their house if I wanted to. I forced myself to switch the phone off; time was tickin' and I needed to save the battery till I got myself a knock off iPhone charger.

Staying here was not an option. I thought about Lancashire, knew a few hiding places. My aunt had a great little cottage just outside Whalley, pretty secluded, middle of nowhere. I wasn't going back inside again.

I bought myself a tent and camping gear from the local Army and Navy down the road. I contacted an old cellmate and, with their money, bought myself a stolen white van with false plates. Then I handed their cards over to him for an extra £50 per card, perfect.

Cheshire was my destination. I needed to see Karen just one more time. Apologise maybe, make sure she was OK. I didn't know how but I had to see her. Her fit little body haunted me. According to Google maps, their house was only two miles from the nearest train station. My mission was on. I loaded all the info I needed onto my phone, got rid of hers out of the car window, straight onto the M60. I was off. I kept local radio on, just in case I was on the news.

What a sleepy little village they lived in, with only one local shop, a church, two pubs and a tiny primary school, sweet. Made me hate him even more. I stopped and bought enough food to keep me going for a few days plus a few bottles of brandy—medicinal purposes of course. At last minute, I grabbed a newspaper off the shelves. Got back in my van and practically tore my way through it. Was he dead? Had I killed the little prick? Hope she was OK, though. I scrolled through—bingo! Page 2 headline:

"Cheshire Couple Shot by Armed Burglar."

Jesus, I was famous again, for all the wrong reasons. So he was still alive, with life-changing injuries. I didn't know what that meant, but at least I hadn't killed the prick. Armed robbery, though, fifteen years inside. I wasn't going back there again. They didn't know who the burglar was. I had a mask on, didn't I. Anyway, if they knew it was me my face would be all over the papers.

I had time to get myself a taste of Cheshire life, to see how the other half lived. With literally my life in the back of the van, I drove nearer to their house.

Finding it was no problem. Thank God it was isolated, just what I wanted, surrounded by fields and woodland. Perfect. I'd wait till it got dark, then have a bit of a mooch around.

It sure was a different world to the drug haven I'd just come from. Within about half a mile, I pitched up my tent, surrounded by thick trees and bushes. No one would find me. I decided to chill, get myself a game plan. It would be a few days until she came home. I only shot her a bit in the foot.

I was right. Four days later, there she was lookin' hot, every inch perfect to me. My heart went out to her when I saw her. I swore I must be goin' soft. She looked so lost, and she was struggling to walk on her crutches. I wanted to speak to her, to help her, to pick her up and carry her in. I was desperate to put my arms around her and tell her I was sorry, that he was the bastard I wanted to hurt, not her.

I couldn't stop myself watching her and her kids. I was

obsessed. I could see them nice and clearly thanks to my binoculars. What a top buy they were! I couldn't get too close though, people kept comin' and goin'. It had to be the fuzz. I wanted to be near her, to touch her and to smell her skin. Seeing her daily, crying, struggling and helpless, I just wanted to put my arms around her and tell her it would be all alright. I had to get a grip. I spent my days imagining she was with me and not him, that complete waste of space she married. This was all his fault. If only I'd had Karen all those years ago instead of Jeanie, would we be together now? They could have been our kids? Maybe she wouldn't have the big flash house, but I would have treated her better than he has, not got her into this fucking mess.

23

Karen

Wednesday 11.45am

Mike pays me another visit. He's been a real godsend. He genuinely seems interested in how me and the girls are coping. He's a bit taller than you, I guess about five foot seven, a lot taller than me. His caring green eyes always seem to pierce right into me.

"Hi Karen, can we sit down somewhere?"

"Yeah, let's go into the lounge. The girls won't hear us from there."

Your mum leaves the room to make us all some tea. Bless her, she brews up for all and sundry, whoever enters the house. I don't think she can handle our situation and it is her way of coping. Mind you, neither can I.

"We think we have a picture of our suspect, but we need to have a chat with you and Will, if that's OK?" Mike looked desperately sorry for me. He's practically a lodger, I've seen him so much recently. He's been amazing. He's been the support that has been lacking from you in all this mess. "Can we go through a couple of questions with you both?"

"Can I see the picture now?"

"To be honest, Karen, we'd rather show you the images together if it's alright."

"Of course, yes. I was going to see him this afternoon, but we can go there now if you need to. I'll just need five minutes to get ready. Have your tea and I'll be down in a minute."

Your dad promised to collect me later, so I set off with the officers Mike and Tracy to meet you at the hospital. DS Stones looks like she's on work experience, or am I getting old? I certainly feel like I've aged lately. They didn't say much to me on the way, but my brain is on overload. I can't stop wondering who it is. Do I really want to see that face again, those eyes? A shiver goes down my spine. I pull my cardigan tight around my waist, trying to keep warm. Even though it's still a heatwave outside, I'm shivering. I squeeze my eyes shut, trying not to recall his stare. I'm absolutely exhausted from another troubled night's sleep and all the stress. I must have nodded off in the back seat. You know me, I always doze off in cars. I wake with a sudden jolt forward. Some teenager has run across the busy road and Tracy has slammed hard on the breaks.

When we arrive on your ward, you are, as predicted, in a low mood. The nursing staff tell me that you are barely eating, only communicating with yes/no answers. They have tried you out of bed, just standing with the Zimmer frame. Not for long though. Apparently you were in agony, feeling faint and vomited on the floor. They reinforce to me that it is going to be a very long process, but to begin with, your mood has to change.

The police go through a few things with both of us.

"We think we know who the suspect is." They show us a CCTV picture from the cash point in Manchester. "We've enhanced the image. We think it's an ex-con called Jeremy

Winter. Do you know anyone by that name?"

You run your fingers through your hair, sweat appears on your top lip and you don't look at all surprised to me. Had you suspected him all along? You'd not mentioned anything—but then again, you haven't said much to me at all! Meanwhile, I am completely horrified to see those eyes.

"Yes, I do!" You try to sit up, which must have jolted your leg judging by the wince on your face. You grab some water from the side table, and you look dreadful as the blood drains from your face. "That little prick went to prison years ago, accused of manslaughter and grooming a minor." The sip of water seems to have helped you collect yourself.

"Yes, we know," the sergeant says. "He's also on the sex offenders list and was released from prison seven months ago. Does he have a grudge against either of you?"

"Would have thought so." You wipe your top lip, which is now beading with sweat, and you shuffle awkwardly in your bed. Bless you, you look so uncomfortable. I want to help but you haven't let me near you for a while now. "I was his area manager and Karen worked for him part-time. I knew he was bad news; that shit has shown his true colours again, hasn't he!"

I can feel my face burning, and my skin begins to crawl. It's hard to breathe. I hadn't recognised him from the photo. On the picture his eyes look so haggard, not how I remembered him.

"We both had to give evidence against him. Jez and I didn't get along from day one. He was a good manager but he'd been given that job far too young. He was a stroppy little shit, especially around me, but his staff all idolised him. His figures were always on the up. As far as a shop manager, he'd done a great job. But we clashed, big time. I knew something wasn't right about him. There was always something odd but I just couldn't put my finger on it, the perverted little paedo. Then my little niece needed a Saturday job, and Jez took her on. I couldn't believe it when I found out he'd been sleeping with her. Even more shocked when we found out she was pregnant. That little bastard got all he deserved; he should have got a murder charge, but they couldn't prove it."

You speak through clenched teeth, the frown line on your forehead deepens and sweat starts to trickle slowly down your temples. You grab a fistful of sheets as if he was there in the room and you want to tear him apart. Shame you didn't do that on the night though, isn't it? Shame you took ages to come to my rescue.

"My brother won't have anything to do with me now, since she died, thanks to that little prick. Him and my sister-in-law partly blame me for Jeanie's death. Where is this little shit now?"

I stare out of the window, trying to compose myself. I'm shaking, my mouth so dry, and a large knot is developing in my stomach.

"We don't know. We have a team on it. We are just waiting for him to make a mistake. He will, it's just a matter of time."

"Is he the one sending me the texts?" I ask in a small voice.

"What fucking texts?" you scream, finally turning your head from the door. "You didn't say he was texting you! How long has that gone on, for God's sake?" Your face is pinched and full of hate.

"Only in the last couple of days. He took my phone, Will, remember?"

"Why were you keeping that quiet?"

"We didn't want to give you anything else to stress about." Mike chipped in.

"Oh, for God's sake, anything else I should know about?"

"We all thought it would be a good idea not to, with your condition at the moment," Mike added. Bless him, even he doesn't know what to say.

DS Stones doesn't quite know where to look either, and hides her fourteen-year-old face behind her mousy hair, which is escaping from a messily constructed ponytail tied awkwardly back.

I take a huge breath and try to compose myself because you're not going to be happy with what I have to say.

"I had a brief fling with him, years ago, way before Will and I got together," I blurt the information out, feeling sick as soon as the words leave my mouth. My head is down. Have I made a huge mistake telling you now? "It was only a fling, Will, I promise. Just three dates. He was my boss. Back in the day he was handsome, fun. Oh, Jesus Christ!"

"What the fuck?"

"Will, I'm so sorry." I'm quivering, my hands holding each arm tight, pulling hard on my sleeves.

"So you knew all along who it was."

"No, Will, of course I didn't."

"Bet you quite liked it, didn't you, him with his hands all over your body, two men fighting over you. You got me shot, you slut!" You spit those words out with such venom, I cower in my chair.

I don't know what else to say. But your face says it all. You're disgusted. Even the police look horrified. I try to grab your hand but you snatch it from me, turning your head to face the door, horror in your eyes, tears streaming down your cheeks.

"Please Will, let me explain."

"Fuck off," is all you can say.

"I worked with Jez for two years," I whisper to Mike and his officer. I can feel them both looking at me. Are they judging or are they just sorry for me? It's difficult to tell but I can't give them eye contact. I keep my eyes firmly on the floor, twisting my hands and feeling momentarily sick. "He was lovely, then." My mouth is so dry. "We had a fling, it was only for three weeks." I'm so embarrassed.

"He was younger than me." I turn to face you but still you stare at the door, zero eye contact. "I called it off after that. I felt awkward him. He was immature and he was a bit odd. I was sure he'd followed me home a few times, which really freaked me out, so I backed off and just told him I wanted to call it all off. As far as being a manager was concerned, he was always fair to me. We all worked hard for him, and he was brilliant at his job. We suspected Jeanie fancied him and did our best to warn him off. He didn't seem keen but she made it so obvious that she was after him." I cough. Mike hands me a glass of water. "To be honest, Jeanie forced herself on him, or it appeared that way. We were all staggered when we found out what had happened. I think Jez is a weak man when it comes to women. It must have gone on for a while. The only obvious change was that Jeanie had gone from an awkward, cocky teenager into a lovely, helpful and sweet girl." I pause for another sip of water. "When we found out that they were together, that's when he became different: arrogant, obnoxious. We had no clue she was pregnant. Thinking back, in the last few weeks before Jeanie died, Jez was foul-tempered with all of us, especially her. He must have known by then that she was having a baby. The last day we saw him though, he was on a high. We'd had a great Saturday, and everything seemed to be back to normal. He was his old self: chirpy, charming, great fun to work for. Until the next time we saw him in court. I've never seen him since. He's gone for revenge and blamed us for his prison time, I suppose," I ramble on, trying to fill the awkward silence.

Mike places his hand on my shoulder. "Did you mention any of this when you were in court?"

"No, no, I didn't think any of this was relevant to the case."

"Jesus Christ, what next?" you mutter under your breath. Apart from that comment, you're speechless and you won't acknowledge me. You run your hands through your hair and wipe sweat from your face.

"Thinking back, the burglar had piercing eyes, and so had Jez, but I'd never put the two together–" I just think of something else and stop dead. "He'd been watching us, I think; my daughter thought she saw someone in the woods that afternoon. Also, at the cabin he said 'your two brats' when he was in our bedroom. I forgot to mention that before. So that's why he kept saying 'You're going to pay' during the attack. I didn't understand it at the time, but it all makes sense now."

I run into your bathroom and throw up. I lean my head against the cool white wall tiles and stay there for a few moments, trying to get a grip, trying to breathe, trying to compose myself. I flush the toilet, splash cold water onto my face and hands, and catch a glance at myself in the mirror. I look dreadful, easily ten years older. My eyes are sunken and my cheeks look hollow and gaunt. I dry myself and return to your room where two pairs of eyes watch my every move. Absolute silence. You look as if you are about to explode, your mouth pulled into a hard line, nostrils flaring as you stare bitterly at the door. You lie there, fuming.

"Well it's not good for me. I need to know *everything* that's going on. Got it!"

I've never seen you this mad before.

"I have another image of Mr Winter. He's been a bit beaten up whilst inside but this is the best picture we have as well as CCTV. Does this ring any bells? I know he was wearing a balaclava but you mentioned you think you see some similarity in his eyes?

A chill goes through me. I am horrified at Jez's transformation.

"Oh God, yes, those eyes, but I'd never have recognised him. He looks like an old man now. He had hair when we knew him. Now he looks gaunt and ravaged. Prison did take its toll on him."

"Still fancy him, do ya?" A sarcastic comment from you that I try to ignore.

Mike clears his throat and collects the paperwork. I can tell he is embarrassed by the way you're treating me. "Well, if you can think of anything else, please don't hesitate to give me a call. You have my card. We have CCTV footage of him at Crewe train station and forensics think they have good fingerprints in your car. We will keep you informed. We know where he lived, but he hasn't been seen for a few days now. He's also broken his parole, which will make it easier for the arrest when we eventually catch up with him."

The door closes gently and you and I sit in an awkward silence for about another ten minutes, until you speak through clenched teeth.

"So, you had a little fling with that tosser, did you? Why did you never tell me? Why the big secret?"

"Because I knew how much you hated him. I decided not to say anything. It wasn't serious and it was way before you and I got together!"

"Did you sleep with him?"

"Yes, twice, but that's all. I told you it wasn't serious."

"Serious enough to sleep with him! Jesus Christ, any more flings I should know about?"

You are absolutely livid and buzz the nurse for pain relief, turning your back on me once again. I have nothing left to say. This is all my fault. My night out at The Midland, my bid for the log cabin. My fault we were burgled. My fault your leg is amputated. My fault our marriage is on the rocks. We sit there in silence for another 45 minutes.

Eventually, I get up and go. I try to kiss you but you turn your head. I wipe my face of tears and leave the room. Your dad is sat reading the newspaper waiting for me. I am unable to speak. He pops in to see you, but he doesn't stay very long either.

"He's really down today, isn't he? He hardly said a word."

"Yes, he's not been good; the police think they know who the suspect is."

Jez has invaded my headspace now. It all comes back to me again and I relive it all. We weren't the only ones to give evidence, so why did he target us? Thinking about it some more, I can't believe he's done this to get back at me. We'd split up on good terms. He was always fair and decent to me after that in the shop, and there was no sign of any animosity. However, you hated Jez from day one, maybe that was the reason why. You gave him such a hard time and it was you that insisted Jez take Jeanie on. If he hadn't employed her he would still probably be working in Manchester, not having done ten years in prison. You are the one with a severe injury, maybe it was you he was after. My wound was only minor compared to yours. Could this be just revenge on you? But why attack all of us? Why not just go after you? Now the kiss makes perfect sense, but when he said he was going to have a bit of rich as well. Oh God, I can't bear to think about it. Maybe he did have plans for me. I shudder at the thought.

Back at home, the girls are waiting; they are so very clingy—understandably—so am I. All I want to do is wrap us all in cotton wool and keep us all safe.

"How's Dad? What did the police want, Mummy?"

"Well, they think they have found the bad man. They were showing us pictures."

Your dad's eyes fix on your mum. "I'll tell you later," he mouths.

"Good. Does that mean he's going to prison?" Ellie asks. Bless her, she's become so protective.

"Yes, hun. If it's him, then he will go to prison for a very long time." I place my hand gently on her head.

"What if it's not him?"

"Try not to worry, Jesse. The police think it's the right man, sweetheart." *They've just got to catch him*, I thought to myself.

Speaking to the police and establishing it could be Jez helps me a bit. I still have questions as to why he targeted us, and so violently. Jez and I parted amicably. I still worked for him for a year after the split. There was never a problem at work. We still had a laugh together. Maybe he did hold a grudge against me, for calling it off all those years ago, but that didn't compare to how awfully you had treated him. I was one of the members of staff who warned him against Jeanie. He knew that I'd started to date you. Maybe he hated me because of that as well, but he was never unpleasant. Maybe it was because we had given evidence in court, but we had to, we had no choice. Perhaps he just needed to take it out on someone. At some point, I still have to tell you about him stalking me, but this isn't the time. I don't think you'd give a damn right now anyway.

You were seething today though; it was written all over your face. You weren't asking me for details. I could imagine you were trying to work it all out on your own. Jez has ruined your life, your leg, maybe now even your marriage. I know you are asking yourself why I dated that prick, what was I thinking. Why had I never mentioned Jez? Why the big secret? In reality, I have no idea why I hadn't told you about him. Maybe I knew you would react the way you did today. You can't believe I'd slept with that 'tosser' as you had so often called him in the past.

You'd got more and more agitated whilst you were having a go. I honestly believed you were going to slap me. Now you hate me even more and the bridge between us is getting ever wider. You buzzed for the nurse in the middle of all your ranting and she asked you if you needed a sedative. "Yeah, get me the whole bottle, and a shotgun, put me out of my misery," had been your reply.

24

Karen

Thursday 2pm, one month later

Four weeks after the attack, as if things couldn't get any worse, our finances are spiralling out of control. We had some savings, but the majority of our funds are tied up with a monstrous mortgage on the house and a commercial mortgage on the business. Bills land daily on the doorstep. I've tried to ignore the rattle of the letterbox. You are the business; it relies solely on you. No Will, no sales, no business—it's that simple.

The medical staff explain that it will take at least three months before you to start to recover, provided you don't go off the rails and have a nervous breakdown. Bills are piling up, but no money is coming in. Instead, expensive Ferraris, Jaguars, and Bentleys are on the forecourt and not going anywhere. If I approach you with any more doom and gloom, I'm convinced it will tip you over the edge. Our belts are going to be well and truly tightened.

So much has happened and is still going on. It is hard for me to decide what our next plan of action should be.

My head is scrambled. You're in such a dark place I have no clue where to turn. I tried to talk to you about the whole Jez fling thing, tried to make peace with you, but all that did was open up already raw wounds. Instead of easing the situation it just made things worse. You threw your cup of water at me and demanded that I leave the room. It's the first clear act of hate I'd ever seen from you. Where do we go from here? I have no idea. What is going to happen to us? Is it over?

Back home, your parents stayed as long as they could, but even they had to get back to their own lives. If I am honest, I need my own space, now more than ever. Our situation is so impossible to sort and such a nightmare to process.

As much as I try to delay it, I know I have to meet with our accountant. Our situation is impossible. I have spoken to the head at the girls' school, explaining our circumstances, but they couldn't give a damn. "If we helped one family, we'd have to help them all," was their response. You always hated them going to a private school, that was another one of my bright ideas, wasn't it!

To cut down on our food bills, the girls and I designed a healthy menu. We cook together; it's fun and a good distraction for us all. We threw away far too much out-of-date food each week anyway, so things had to change. I had to let the cleaner and the gardener go a few weeks ago. So now we have enough savings to last us for about eight weeks. We are asset rich, cash poor. All our funds are tied up in both our properties.

We went way over the top with our house, didn't we—it was ridiculously luxurious. Did we really need the five bedrooms, seven bathrooms? The orangery extension alone cost the price of a small house. The three acres of manicured gardens were a great idea at the time, but it took so much energy to maintain. Also, there were the treble garages with two outhouses that were never used.

When I add up all that money we wasted, I wish we'd saved or invested at least some of it. That would have been a blessing now. But we didn't, did we. We were flamboyant. The stone hallway floor that you insisted we bought, although that was another fortune, always worries the life out of me. I am constantly fretting and telling the girls to be careful; should any of us fall from that wooden staircase, it would be fatal. But you wanted to make an impression the moment people walked into our house. Appearances matter to you.

Did we really need that expensive interior designer? No, we could have had fun doing all the work ourselves. No expense had been spared though, had it, on an eclectic mix of old and new furniture, and quirky finishing touches. Yes, it looks amazing. But the excessive amount of money spent on our curtains alone ran into the thousands. Ellie's bedroom with her *Pirates of the Caribbean* theme: sails for curtains, fish netting dotted around the room, and various old-fashioned props to emulate the boat. Jess's room with its modern twist on Cinderella: a castle-shaped bed and two life-size cartoon caricatures of the ugly sisters painted on the wall. The girls were only five when we moved in. We went to town on their rooms, desperate that they should feel safe in their new surroundings. The kitchen and bathrooms: did we need to have state of the art, digital mood electrics and lighting? The old cellar with its cinema room, with your games room towards the rear; you only used that room once, the night Ted and Alice came round. Every inch of our house is superb, without a doubt.

No expense had been spared with an attention to the very finest of details. Out on the driveway the triple garage with office space above, where you insisted you would work from home, but you never did. That alone would have made a great two bedroomed house. The stables have been modernised for storing a couple of vintage cars: one silver Rolls Royce, and a classic red e-type Jag. We didn't need these cars; they were only driven two or three times a year. We have undoubtedly made this place a dream home and it is beautiful, but it took us five years to complete. We didn't need to spend all that money. If only we'd saved some of it, not gone over the top, we would have more funds available now in our bank account, something for that rainy day.

The meeting with the accountant is depressing, but I knew it wasn't going to be an upbeat conversation. His initial suggestion is to get both the house and your business property valued as soon as, just in case we need to sell them quickly. He also advises us to maybe get an inventory list of the more expensive items around the house: paintings, all my expensive jewellery (although most of my things were stolen by Jez—which reminds me, I need to get that insurance claim in as you've insisted, at least that would give us some cash in the bank for a while.) There may be a possibility of auctioning them. He proposes downsizing the cars to more practical vehicles for both of us, and yours will have to be adapted or automatic to accommodate your leg. You are not going to be a happy man when you hear all of this. Any private lessons for the girls are going to have to go. The twins haven't been in the mood to go to any lately anyway. I need to find some freelance work. It seems like a decade ago that me and Louise shared a meaty graphics project, only months really, but so much has gone on. I could do with seeing Louise. Seems like a lifetime ago we had a good laugh together, and she'd cheer me up.

Your PA, Lois, is becoming ever more concerned. She totally threw me when we had coffee together.

"Karen, sales have been slow now for eighteen months. This is not a new thing. Even if Will wasn't in hospital, we would be having this conversation. Business has gone downhill rapidly, I thought you knew. I'm sorry. Bills are mounting up and no cars are being sold. Will is our only sales force."

"Oh my God, why didn't he tell me? I thought everything was going well. He never gave any inclination that things were so bad."

Poor Lois, she was concerned about her job too. She hadn't been paid, her last two cheques had bounced and apparently, you had told her not to worry. Lois didn't want to leave, she didn't want to let you down, but she had her own bills to pay.

I hadn't expected any of this. It's hard to get my head around it, with the emotional and physical damage. Not to mention Mum. Is this rock bottom or is there more to come?

I have started to drive again, thank God, and my car—fortunately at the moment—is an automatic. It was an immense relief to have some form of freedom back, even though I am accompanied by the police, but that can't go on for much longer. They can't protect us forever. We have to discuss the house, the sooner the better, but I'm struggling to get us both talking about general things, let alone this financial mess. You totally ignore me now when I visit. I actually dread seeing you. My fling with Jez has tipped you well and truly over the edge.

Another thing is that, at some point, Mum's apartment needs to be cleared. Jenny from social services and I have decided it is best for her to remain in the residential, she's safe and happy there. So she has to sell her place to pay for the residential fees.

After the meetings with the accountant and the PA, I decide to give myself a break for the weekend. I am desperate to spend time with the girls, just try to maintain some normality—if that is ever to be possible again. They are showing small signs of improvement, although their nightmares continue to haunt them. They follow me everywhere around the house, like they did when they were toddlers. My foot is healing nicely but still gives me pain now and then, particularly last thing at night. The house is now a lot more secure against any possible intruders, which gives me some peace of mind.

It is looking like you'll be home in the next week or so, if you continue to make progress. We're all extremely worried about you. Although you're putting on a brave front with the nursing staff, we're all too aware that something's not right. Despite physical improvements, your moods are still unpredictable, especially where I'm concerned. Any former trace of romance has gone. Every time you see me without your parents or the girls you bring up Jez and my fling. You hate me, you blame me for everything. Our marriage is a total mess and I feel there is no hope, but the more you push me away the more desperate I become. If I am honest, you frighten me. With Jez still on the loose, I feel like I'm going to lose it any day soon.

The weekend goes as well as could be expected, considering. Before we know it, the girls are back at school. We are paid up until the end of term so that gives me a couple of months to find them a new school. Now it is time to face the music. The estate agent calls on Monday and he sets about valuing the house. It's so depressing, seeing our dream home being categorised, measured and photographed room by room.

"Oh yes, Karen, we'll have no problem selling this, it's beautiful!" he proudly exclaims, thinking he's doing me a favour. *Yes, I know*, I say to myself, *our hearts and souls went into this place*. "No problem at all selling this."

If we sell it, we will have enough money to buy a smaller house outright. The garage property is also valued, and the small amount made on this would give us an income for approximately six months tops, if we're frugal. It's not the ideal scenario, but the valuations are better than I'd thought. That's some good news for a change.

I just need to have the discussion with you and I'm dreading it. You have always hankered after a monster of a house, building your empire. I wasn't bothered, a small family home would have done me, it didn't matter as long as we were happy. Still, with everything going on, moving house and starting afresh is ever more appealing to me these days.

It is almost like you are psychic, that you know exactly what I am going to say, and immediately go on the defensive.

"We are not selling the bloody house. Do you hear me?" you bellow. "No way! I can work from here if I have to!"

"Hun, if we carry on the way we are going, in three months we will be repossessed and lose them both." There it was, the information was out there.

"It won't happen that quickly, Karen."

"I know you've not been selling cars for months. Lois has told me all about it. Why didn't you tell me? There's never been secrets between us, so why now?" The minute I say it I know it is a mistake.

"Wasn't Jez a secret?" you practically spit at me through gritted teeth.

I fear you are going to hit me. The damning look is frightening. Your eyes glaze over and you turn your head in your petulant manner, now a common sight. You say nothing. I take a deep breath despite your verbal attack. I'm not letting this one go.

"I've spoken to the accountant. If the mortgages don't get paid after three months, they start court proceedings."

"They're always negative!"

I am bashing my head against a brick wall here and getting nowhere. In the middle of our heated discussion, the surgeon walks in, not realising the mammoth row he has interrupted.

"Hi Will, Karen, how's it going?"

"Ah great Doc, thanks." Your demeanor changes,

showing evidence of the existence of the old Will in that body somewhere, with your warm, friendly smile, the smile I haven't seen since that Saturday evening . You're making me so desperately unhappy. All I want is a small iota of a sign that you still have any feelings for me.

When visiting time is over, I ask to speak to your surgeon again. He's concerned too.

"Will was far too chirpy; he's covering up his feelings. The nursing staff have mentioned that Will is always laughing and joking and yet there are numerous references from the nurses about his state of mind. He's mister sweetness and light. He's not showing any of the upset or anger that we would normally expect to see with his condition."

I try to explain how dire things are at home and when we are alone together. That he's holding something back. "He won't even look at me anymore."

The surgeon agrees that if you're not careful, you are heading for a major nervous breakdown.

"The antidepressants appear to be working, as far as we're concerned. You obviously know him better than us, so medically he can probably go home next week. He will still need to have regular physio and keep up his exercises, but he won't be able to work for a long time, particularly with the stress he is under. Was he under a lot of pressure at work before the attack?"

"He's always had stressful jobs, and he's always worked at least twelve-hour shifts ever since I've known him. We used to joke about the fact that he was no spring chicken anymore. It was about time he slowed down. I'm afraid he has always been a workaholic. I thought there wasn't a problem at work," I lower my voice, "but his PA has told me last week his business has been failing for months. He never told me any of this. Will has always been able to cope with an enormous amount of stress, it's who he is, but he's been keeping this from me."

"I understand, but he's also been brutally attacked and he probably thought you were going to be killed that night. He's been under enormous emotional as well as physical strain, as have you all. Think of it as post-traumatic stress disorder, the depression that soldiers get after a tour of duty. Put an amputated limb on top of all that and you have a man on the edge. I'm not trying to worry you; I just want you to be aware. Keep an eye out for any further signs. Let me talk to him as well."

"Thank you. I'll arrange for the accountant to see him as well, see if that makes him take it all a bit more seriously."

"Hold back with the accountant, if you can for a week. Let's not give him any more negativity for the time being. I'll go and have a word with him now, you get yourself home."

"Thank you," I reply with a weak smile.

Now every time I see you, you manage to reduce me to tears and I just don't know what to do.

As I race (as quickly as I can) to the car to collect the girls from the bus, my mobile rings. It's the residential home. Mum has had a fall and been taken to hospital—ironically, here, the same one as yours. *I don't bloody believe it!* I think to myself. *Christ, can this get much worse?*

I phone Louise to see if she can pick the kids up for an hour, get back out of the car and hobble down the other end of the corridor to the medical ward—it feels like miles away—this time to see my mum. My foot is throbbing like crazy by the time I get there, and my head is about to explode, another migraine looming. Fortunately, my handbag contains half the pharmacy these days and there's a couple of headache tablets in there. *Jesus, someone up there help me, please just give me a break.*

Mum is in the side ward, lying unconscious. An enormous bruise extends over one half of her face.

"Bless you, Mum, I'm here." I kiss her forehead gently, careful not to hurt her. She looks so small, so frail, her skin is shiny and doll-like. In her left arm there's a drip. They'd clearly struggled with her veins because her hand is all colours of the rainbow. She's covered in bruises. *Oh for goodness sake, how much more can I have thrown at me?* I haven't prayed in over four years, but this time I sit down and put my hands together in that pose reminiscent of childhood days. I'm way overdue for this, but I speak to God anyway. Someone has to help me.

The doctor explains that she will be scanned tomorrow morning. They are going to observe her overnight. "I suggest you go home. We know all about your unfortunate situation. Get some sleep and hopefully she'll be awake in the morning. The next 24 hours are crucial, but try not to worry, she's in good hands."

"You really have no clue just how unfortunate and dire my situation is!" I mutter under my breath.

Reluctantly, and under their instructions, I take what seems to be an extremely long and painful walk back to the car and drive home on autopilot. Louise gives me a huge hug as I sob in her arms—yet again. She has become my only lifeline. Bless her, she's bought us all a takeaway and there they are, all four kids sat on the lounge floor tucking into Hawaiian pineapple pizza and garlic bread in front of a *Shrek* DVD. She pours me a huge glass of white wine while I try my utmost to explain my ever-evolving nightmare, which is rapidly spiralling out of control.

"Can it get any worse? If I wrote a book about it, no one would believe me!"

There is no reply from Louise, but she's a comfort.

All four kids have a whale of a time, totally unaware of our new developments. It's good to see them having fun for once. Louise stays for a couple of hours. I offload. She has become my counsellor.

"Well, one day, maybe you should write a book about all this, because it's such a series of unfortunate events. It's a bestseller!" No matter how dreadful all this gets, she is the one person who can still make me laugh.

"The one time I could do with Will by my side, he's got so much crap of his own to deal with. I don't have the spare time to keep up with the day-to-day stuff, let alone my mum, the girls, Will, Will's nervous breakdown, and my foot, which is bloody killing me by the way." Poor Louise is speechless for once against the tidal wave of my sad little life. "He's blaming me for this whole mess, I know he is. The fling with Jez, he'll never forgive me for that, the weekend away. I see him cringe every time I walk into his room. I just don't know what I can do to make things better."

Louise puts an arm around me. "Time will heal, but you have so many things yet to overcome. Just be patient. It will happen, trust me, it just takes time."

"I don't think it ever will. He's losing it, he's heading for a nervous breakdown and I don't know how to deal with that either. Why us? We're not bad people. I'm a goody two shoes, for God's sake. I've never done a thing wrong in my life. I'm so sorry to offload all this on to you yet again, you must be sick of me."

"Hey, that's what good friends are for. One day I will need you, that's how it works, OK? So don't hold back anymore, or otherwise Will won't be the only one having a breakdown. One of you needs to keep it together."

Three large glasses of wine later, I tell the girls to go and get ready for bed. Louise and her kids leave. I am alone.

I must have been crying in my sleep, as the following morning my eyes are swollen and practically glued together. I look and feel dreadful. The thought of sorting out Mum's apartment is at the back of my mind, but I just can't bring myself to go there.

Visiting hours at the hospital are from 11 in the morning, so I get there at 11 on the dot with my policeman in tow. This is the last place I want to be right now. It is time to speak to yet another doctor, this time about Mum's fall. The staff take me into a private waiting room, never a good sign. I prepare myself for yet more tragic news.

"What now?" I hold my head in my hands, elbows leaning firmly on my knees.

"Karen, we have scanned your mum this morning and she has a severe bleed on the brain due to her fall. There is quite a considerable amount of swelling. All we can do now is wait the next few days to see if she regains consciousness. Her age is against her and, if I'm honest, it's not looking good. We must advise you to prepare for the worst. We just need to wait and see what happens next. I'm sorry it's more bad news. Do you have anyone who can spend time with you?"

"I have my kids. I don't have time to spend with anyone else except them at the moment."

The nurse standing next to the doctor has her head tilted to one side. She looks so sorry for me. Her next sentence absolutely floors me.

"What about your brother? He was here earlier."

"But … I don't have a brother. You must have the wrong room."

"No, it was definitely this room. The nurse filling in your mum's chart spoke to him. Maybe she misheard him. She said he was your brother, lovely blue eyes, a lot older than you."

"Jesus! I don't believe it, it can't be…"

I glare at the policeman and my face says it all. He's immediately in the corridor on his mobile. I guess he's phoning Mike.

"He left those flowers."

The card has ten kisses on it. It is covered in hearts. The blood drains from my head and I'm grabbed by the nurse.

"Put your head between your knees, lovey, you look like you're going to faint."

She passes me a glass of water and I try to get my head together.

"Take some deep breaths, sweetheart."

"What did he look like?" I ask, panicked.

"I'm sorry, I don't know, apart from the blue eyes. I'll get the nurse who was here at the time. She said he didn't stay long."

The staff nurse appears within minutes. "A man in his fifties was here, only about fifteen, twenty minutes ago."

"What did he look like?" I quiz the staff nurse this time.

"As I say, age about fifty, grey receding hair, lovely blue eyes. I'm sure he said he was your brother otherwise we wouldn't let him in. He seemed younger when he spoke."

"Christ, no! It's him. I don't have a brother," I repeat, dazed and shaking, whispering the latter part of the sentence to my police escort who has come back and is listening intently.

"OK love, I'm just going to organise another officer to be outside this room for your mum as well. I'll stay till someone turns up."

The next hour is spent just watching Mum. She looks radically different from the pampered person I saw only a few days ago. I try to take a few bites of a cheese sandwich and a hot drink from the staff nurse but it sticks in my throat.

It takes all my energy to visit you on the other side of the hospital. Still in shock, desperately lonely, yet knowing full well I won't share this latest piece of information with you. What's the point? You don't care anymore; you'd find some excuse to shout at me and I just can't cope with that today.

The staff had you up and about for the first time on a Zimmer frame; apparently, you had been doing pretty well. That was, however, until you saw me. Your pyjama leg on

159

the amputated side has been pinned up so you wouldn't trip. You stand bent on your one good leg. I watch you for a while from by the nurses' station, out of sight. As you struggle to get halfway down the corridor you see my face and scream out loud like a child, breaking down in tears. You're hysterical. This is not how you wanted me to see you. You hobble back up to the ward and then throw yourself on the bed like a spoiled teenager.

"I told you not to get me up yet, I told you!" you bellow at the student nurse. "I specifically told her—" You point at the young girl accusingly and my heart goes out to her, she's only doing her job "—I told you to leave me till the evening. I didn't … I didn't want you to see me like this … ever! Christ, what the fuck's happened to me, to us? What did we do to deserve this? Why did this happen? Why, Karen? Why?"

It's the first time I've seen you behave like this, but it's also the first time in weeks that you've called me Karen and acted like you care. I try to hug you but you push me away

On your side table are a few unopened cards.

"Is it OK if I have a look at these?" I ask you, trying to calm things down by changing the subject, but you have your head thrust into the pillow like a child and ignore me.

In the past I've always opened your mail. The first one stops me in my tracks. It's a 'With Deepest Sympathy' card and I dread opening it, knowing too well who it's from. I just know.

Mike must be psychic, because he suddenly appears behind me. He puts his hand on my shoulder.

"Karen—"

He's about to say more but I hand him the card, too scared to read what's inside.

25

Karen

Friday 4.40pm

I drive back home like someone possessed; I need to
see my kids. Mike is crouched behind me on the back
seat. My car screeches onto the gravel drive and I park it
straight into the garage. With Jez visiting my mother that
afternoon, and delivering the sympathy card to you, the
police are now concerned that he has become way too
confident. Mike has assigned two more officers to stay by
your side, as well as Mum's. It's all become too much. I
rush into the kitchen and hold our girls tight.

"What is it, Mummy?" They can tell, they're not stupid

Your parents have arrived for the weekend and they
usher us into the dining room, as it's the only place in the
house that's void of any windows. They were informed of
the situation by the police as we sped home. They have
cooked chicken casserole, our favourite. It's their attempt
to build us up, bring some normality back into our lives.
They hand me an enormous glass of white wine–I'm
drinking far too much of this just lately.

None of us can eat, pushing the food around our plates and staring blankly at the TV screen. Nothing much is said. With more officers assigned to us, they are now patrolling the neighbourhood in unmarked cars. They're on high alert waiting for Jez to make a move, prepared for an imminent disaster. Mike briefs his plainclothes officers in a far corner of the kitchen, out of hearing range.

Your parents leave after tea under police advice; two less people to protect I guess. The evening drags by and at half past eight I'm completely shattered, so me and the girls go upstairs to watch TV on our bed. Mike nods his head goodnight as we leave the room then returns to watching out of the window. All three of us huddle together and drift in and out of sleep. I am even more on edge now; each door and window had been meticulously checked at least three times.

At approximately ten o'clock, a thud from downstairs jolts me from my sleep. I tiptoe out of bed towards the window and peer carefully through the curtains, desperate not to be seen from the outside. The gate is swinging menacingly, open and shut, open and shut, open and shut, creaking. Moonlight casts a streak of light across the top of the bedroom ceiling, just enough to fill the room with a limited flicker. Apart from the gate, everywhere is still. It's eerily quiet. This room is stifling hot but there's no way I'm opening a window tonight, or ever again for that matter, not until this madman is locked up.

As I turn to get back into bed I stop dead—instinct. I know something is wrong. The floorboard on the top step creaks. Am I imagining it? I shake my head as though to banish the thought. No, because there it goes again, another creak. 'Stop it,' I whisper to myself, 'the police are downstairs.' Maybe it was Mike leaving? He promised to stay until 11. Whatever or whoever it is, they are definitely outside our twins' bedroom and I know exactly where. It's the dodgy floorboard, the one we never fixed, so we would always know if the girls were out of their beds.

A dark shadow crosses the light on the hallway wall. A figure is reflected in my dressing table mirror. My heart is lodged firmly in my throat. I swallow hard, purse my lips and breathe through my nose, desperate not to make a sound. I hold my breath and stand rigid, my chest rising and falling in absolute terror. Slowly, I turn to watch the girls as they sleep, completely unaware, undisturbed, with not a care. Knots twist tight in the pit of my stomach. Trying desperately to stifle my panicked breath, I clench my teeth, quietly grab the nearest heavy object—a large square perfume bottle, your Christmas present to me. In three careful strides I'm behind the bedroom door, hidden, cushioned against our dressing gowns hanging from the hooks. I take a deep breath and hold it. Grasping the bottle against my chest with my trembling hands, every inch of my body is bristling in sheer trepidation.

The endless laboured footsteps creep towards our bedroom, towards us. It is him. It's got to be. Where are the police? Why are they not here? I peer through the crack between the door and the frame; that familiar receding hairline from the mug shot and the stench. I can smell him from here. I have no doubt it's him! He walks straight past me, towards my girls, towards my babies, completely unaware that I'm directly behind him.

With all the strength I can muster I lunge hard at the back of his head with the perfume bottle gripped firmly in my hands, sending him groaning to the floor. Is he out? Is he unconscious? Have I killed him? I stand over him, ready to lash out again with my weapon. There's no movement. I lean closer to check him, to see if he is breathing.

He grabs the back of my knee, forcing me to the ground, dragging me on top of him. I try to scream but nothing comes from my mouth.

"Karen, what are you doing?" he pleads in disbelief.

"Don't do this to us."

To us? What's he on about? He's delusional! It's impossible to scramble off him because his spider-like limbs are groping all over, trapping me. He restrains my hands and the perfume bottle rolls under the bed. My only weapon, gone. His slippery sweat is all over me and it makes me gag. He's on top of me, pinning me down, grabbing large handfuls of my hair to keep my head in place. Inhumane eyes stare directly into mine. He tries to push his mouth against mine, no balaclava this time, just a sharp unshaven chin. He's forcing himself upon me, yet again. I whip my head right, pressing my cheek hard against the floor, trying to be as far away as possible from him. Desperate to find the perfume that's rolled under the bed, a weapon, anything, I kick and scratch at any part of him that is near. There's blood: his, mine I can't tell. My hand pads desperately under the bed and finally touches the cool glass of the perfume bottle. He isn't getting me again, or my girls.

They wake!

"Mummy, Mummy!"

He turns his gaze from me to look at my gorgeous girls clinging to one another on the bed and his mouth creases into a crooked smile. My chance to grab the perfume.

With a burst of strength I had no idea I possessed, I lunge hard at his head again, spraying perfume into his eyes, then hit him, over and over, like someone demented.

"Karen, stop." He's cowering. "Ahhh stop! Karen please don't do this to us. I want you—"

"What?" He's insane.

Our girls are screaming and their distress gives me a further burst of strength. He lies still, but I continue to hit him over and over, his blood splattering up my arms, on my face, up the wall.

"Karen!"

Two solid hands are firm on my shoulders. It's Mike,

and he too is covered in blood, his face is dripping. He gently prizes my fingers from my weapon and pulls me firmly to my feet, holding me steady, embracing me. I look at Jez on the floor, his chest is barely moving.

He's groaning through bloodied lips, almost a whisper, "Why Karen, why?" And then he is silent.

"He's dead! Jesus, I've killed him. I never meant to kill him."

Blue flashing lights splay across the ceiling. It is over. Jez's body lies by my dressing table; blood has poured from his left eye and the back of his head and is pooling on the cream carpet.

Mike holds me and the girls tight, the three of us wrapped in his arms as we all sob. It's over, at last. We've got him. I look down at Jez with a sense of relief and a strange sort of calm, then prod him with my foot just to make sure. "He won't harm us now," I reassure my girls.

With a sharp intake of breath, Jez grabs the back of my knee and bellows, "Why?"

In slow motion, I feel myself getting dragged back down to the floor, the girls' hysterical sobs in the background. Mike reacts immediately. He tears Jez's hand from my leg and puts himself firmly between us. He's full of fury as he delivers a resounding blow to Jez's face, sending him reeling back, then roughly rolls him to his side and cuffs him.

26

Karen

Saturday Morning 10.30am

The following morning is as though a page in our life has turned. At last I can open the windows wide, and crisp clean air flows freely throughout the house. Outside, the birdsong is deafening, the grass smells sweet and it looks like it's going to be another glorious day. With Jez captured, I have an overwhelming sense of elation, of freedom and for a brief moment in time I'm smiling. However, my face clouds as memories of the previous night return.

Jez was rushed to hospital and gained consciousness in the ambulance. Mike told me that he was crying and calling for me the whole way, asking why I wasn't with him. Insane! However, even the thought of Jez doesn't stop me from appreciating this beautiful morning, and a glimmer of a smile returns as I close my eyes and listen to the birds. I won't allow him to spoil this glorious day.

As usual, it's all short lived though, isn't it! It's Mum who needs me now. She's still unconscious and deteriorating rapidly. I should have spent more time with her recently and I'm racked with guilt.

When I'm back on her ward my thoughts return to 'Is this it? Is this how she ends her life, after a stupid fall, of all things.' With her age and the Alzheimer's, things aren't looking good and the doctors take me to one side and suggest that the drip should be removed.

"Her brain has showed no signs of functioning, the swelling hasn't reduced, and she isn't demonstrating any signs of recovery." Even though I'm expecting bad news, it still comes as a shock to hear it.

I know in my heart what Mum would have wanted. I know that once the drip is removed, with no food or water, it would just be a matter of days before her organs shut down, only days for me to say goodbye. I just need more time. I can't make a decision yet. I've only just got used to her being in a home, for God's sake. I need time, so no decisions yet. I want it to be just me and Mum.

I brush her hair, apply Vaseline on her dried, cracked mouth and freshen up her face with a cool clean wipe. Her dry hands and arms get a massage with her favourite Chanel No 5 cream, any excuse just to hold her hands. She smells lovely and she looks so peaceful despite her enormous bruise. I stay for a while, until the night draws in, then give her a kiss on her forehead as I leave. I have no intention of seeing you today, I just want to be with my girls.

I decide to go to Mum's apartment. Why, I don't know. Is it a good idea? Maybe it could be somehow cathartic. The girls are off to Louise's house tonight and stopping over. I have time to grieve, even though she's still alive. I just want to try to process everything: you, the attack, our marriage, and now Mum's condition. When is this going to end? If this is character building, then I'm all out of character.

The social worker has organised for the apartment to be superficially cleaned. It isn't her job normally, but Jenny has done it out of sympathy, I guess. The fridge has been emptied and scrubbed. Mum's food had been permanently out of date lately. She had been living off bananas and ham sandwiches. The bins, thankfully, are bleached and any rubbish in them has been put out for the refuse collectors. The toilets have been cleaned and anything that smelled has been thrown away at my request.

The apartment looks huge somehow, without my mother's presence, and bursting with memories of the past years with both my parents. I can almost feel them here next to me. I'm taken back to her last day here, when her own daughter double-crossed her and put her into a care home. She was dressed so smart, hoping to see the doctor. Waves of guilt, shame and grief overcome me and I fall on the floor. It's only weeks but it seems like a lifetime ago since we'd last been here together. I sit cross-legged on the floor, like a small child, clutching a clump of soggy tissues in one hand, unable to move or function.

"OK, come on, this isn't going to get anything done now is it, sweetheart, pull yourself together," my dad says with comforting tones from somewhere beyond this world.

I switch the kettle on, put teabags ready into the pot, and my eyes are drawn to her homemade black and yellow-striped tea cosy. I'm amazed that she hung on to my Mother's Day present to her from twenty years ago, I can't believe she kept this tatty old thing. As I wait for the kettle to boil, I dry my eyes with some fresh kitchen roll and wander around as I try to get a grip on everything, to drum up some motivation from somewhere, anywhere. At some point, I have the task of clearing it myself, or organising a company to take all this away. The latter option probably makes a lot more sense given everything else that is going on. But I can't bear the thought of strangers rifling through their belongings. What the hell am I going to do with it all?

Finding a pen and paper in the kitchen drawer, I start to make notes. The more I think about it, the pros and cons, a clearance company is going to have to do large portion of this for me. I am in no fit state to do it in my present frame of mind. The kettle whistles and snaps me out of my indecision. The teapot is filled and the old knitted tea cosy is placed gently over the top.

Looking around, it saddens me how Mum has left these rooms, the absolute chaos and confusion. Things that belonged in the kitchen were housed in the bathroom, things from the bathroom were in her bedroom. Thank God Jenny's girls cleared the majority of it. Poor old Mum! Saying old—she isn't, by any means, but Alzheimer's has ravaged her in the past seven years. Instead of being a healthy 68-year-old, she's like a confused woman in her eighties, especially in her present condition.

I find a tin in the bedroom and when I open it the smell knocks me back. She's stuffed it with some used wet underwear, probably out of embarrassment. This is going to take a very long time. Her bank book is under her pillow and has three thousand pounds in it from unspent pension money over the past two years. Before anyone comes in to clear the place, I am going to have to sift through everything, but I just can't face it right now. Anyway, I need to get to bed so I can spend as much time with her tomorrow. After two hours of drifting aimlessly from one room to another, I leave for home.

The house is empty. Louise offered to have the girls for a sleepover, so it's a real treat to be alone and have some peace. I can't be bothered to cook or eat so I settle for a five-minute stir fry, and force it down me while I watch TV in bed. At this rate, antidepressants will be dished out to me too, if I'm not careful. *Fawlty Towers* is on, it's the one where Manuel has a rat called Basil and it is the first time in months something has made me laugh; so much so that four episodes down the line my spirits are lifted. "OK, if I can manage to do this every evening for maybe an hour, there might be a light at the end of the tunnel for me," I say out loud to an empty room. A bit of escapism—for a few hours at least—never hurt anyone.

The house alarm is set. It's a good habit the girls and I have adopted and I will keep it up even if Jez is under lock and key. Who knows what other crazy people from my past are out there!

I sleep like a baby until about ten, the longest time in weeks. I'm groggy yet starving, so prepare myself a boiled egg which bubbles away on the hob whilst I dig into my handbag for painkillers as my foot is killing me. I run a nice bubble bath, make myself a huge coffee, and once my breakfast is eaten, I soak for one glorious hour. But niggling at the back of my mind is that decision I need to make for Mum.

Whilst drying myself with one of our huge bath towels, the posh ones I usually keep for guests, the phone rings.

"Hi, it's Louise. The kids are safely at school, and I just wanted to see if you would like me to come to the hospital with you?"

"Thank you, you're an angel. I'd love that."

"I'll pick you up and drop you back after you and I have had some lunch, agreed?"

"Agreed."

"I'll be there in an hour."

"You're a star!" Tears start to form at my friend's thoughtfulness. *Get a grip, get a grip girl*, I tell myself. *Today is the start of a new day.*

Louise is horrified to see the size of the bruise on Mum's face, and seeing her motionless in the bed breaks my heart. I'm envious because Louise's parents are both alive, fit and live life to the full. It must be hard for her to imagine the pain I'm going through, or indeed anything that's happened in the past few months—and yet she has been a rock.

"Karen, have you lot had any serious counselling yet?" She's concerned, taking in the enormity of it all.

"One day, it's on my extensive wish list when I get a spare five minutes."

"Do you want me to organise someone to do a home visit for you and the girls? I have a very good friend, she's amazing! I didn't want to say anything before, but now I really think you need it."

"Yes, that sounds perfect. When … if this is ever over, I owe you big time. You're on a major trip to Portugal: just me, you and our kids.

"Now there's a bloody good idea. I'm going to hold you to that one!"

Just being here with a Louise is a tonic. I have absolutely no desire to visit you at all today, I just want to spend my time with Mum. These are precious moments with her right now. Decisions have to be made, but for the time being I want to stay here.

"Now, let's go see that grumpy git of a husband of yours, shall we. Maybe we can cheer him up a bit."

"That's not going to happen; he hates me."

"Come on. Up you get." She practically drags me up from my seat. "If you like, I can bollock him for you, knock some sense into him. How does that sound?" Her hand is firmly on her hip and she is pointing her finger at an imaginary Will in the corner.

"Ah Louise, just move in with me, I feel better already," I say. I'm honestly dreading being anywhere near you.

"Before we go, what do you think I should do?" I whisper discreetly before kissing Mum's forehead.

"Maybe ask yourself what she would want?" She places both hands on my shoulders, with sadness in her eyes.

"Yep, I've done that."

"And?"

171

"Let's talk outside. Bye, Mum, see you in the morning. Love you." A huge tear trickles down my cheek, which I manage to catch in my hand before Louise sees it.

"I cannot thank you enough for coming here with me today; it's been so much nicer with you around. You've really made my day."

"Well, I've put some deadlines back, and am free now for the next ten days. How about we do this every day, even if we come in two cars? I'm here for you ... OK?" she suggests as we walk out into the corridor. Her hand rests on my shoulder and she pulls me close.

"Thanks, hun. Love you, you really are a good friend." She's been such a huge part of my support mechanism lately; she's filled the enormous gap between you and I. I don't think I'd have coped half as well without her. "The doctors have said Mum has no brain function and if they take the drip out..." the tears nip the back of my nose "... she will last about one week to ten days... I think I know what I have to do." My hands cover my face, and I just can't say the words. I sob uncontrollably in Louise's arms.

"Do you want me to find a doctor for you?"

"Yes, come on, let's do this." I look back through the small window at Mum dwarfed in the hospital bed. She's so tiny.

"Listen, your mum wouldn't have wanted to be a burden, you know that."

Together, we speak to the doctor. He explains the events ahead and it's agreed that the drip will be removed tomorrow morning. The decision has been made. Between us, we will sit with Mum around the clock and keep vigil. Heartbroken, I hold tight to Louise on the way out.

"Come on, let's go and see if we can get a sandwich and a coffee down you, shall we?"

After a brief stop at the hospital café where I just about manage a coffee and a biscuit, we make our way up to visit you.

There you are as usual, sober in mood and slumped in your wheelchair when we arrive. You look terrible. I don't think you've even brushed your hair, let alone shaved. The nursing staff have put you back into a side ward, on your own. Louise's face says it all. I can see she's staggered by how gaunt you are. Your appearance has changed dramatically since she last saw you. You've always been so smart but lately you're looking like an unkempt old man in his late fifties. I understand how traumatic all this has been for you, it has been for us all, but you could at least try to brush your hair.

You fall into the familiar pattern of being Mr sweetness and light to everyone except me. Your face contorts the minute you see me walk in and yet you beam at Louise. You won't look me in the eye—I'm embarrassed by your reaction.

I try to explain Mum's situation, but you're not listening, you couldn't give a damn. You are trapped in Will's world, in your own self-pity, it's all about you. I mean, we were never in that attack with you, were we Will? No matter how nasty you are, I still want to wrap my arms around you.

The next hour is painfully slow. Even Louise, who normally isn't short of her words, is struggling to hold a conversation with you. You're great with her to begin with, until you start to realise that she has so much sympathy for me. It's like you blame her as well because she's my best friend and is my support mechanism. To be honest, I think you're just rude lately, the only people you're relatively normal with are your parents and the nursing staff. You don't even acknowledge our girls. I hold back the tears because I refuse to cry in front of you anymore and I don't want to upset Louise. She doesn't deserve to be in the middle of this. I need you right now and yet you turned your cheek so that I kiss you there instead of your lips when we arrived. You're breaking my heart and I'm at my wits' end.

After a painfully long hour I can stand it no more. This time, I leave without saying goodbye.

"He's gone from me, hasn't he?" I'm in bits.

"How many antidepressants is he on?"

"Not half as many as the ton he needs. Trouble is, I need them too, every time I see him! I've lost him ... the old Will that I loved is gone. I get that he's going through the mill right now, but I'm here for him, I really am. He just keeps pushing me away, and the more he pushes, the harder I try. I've tried to put myself in his shoes. Am I being selfish here? Louise, he's not asked me once how me and the girls are. Anything could have happened to me that night. I know my injuries are nothing compared to his but he won't let me anywhere near him. He detests me, it's written all over his face. Ironic, isn't it. I have a husband that won't speak to me, a mother, bless her, that can't speak to me, and some idiot psychopathic stalker who's been desperate to be with me. Thank God he's locked up."

She gives me a warm hug and leads me back to the car, her arm weaved through mine.

"I'll drop you back. Why don't you have another soak in the bath, stick another sitcom on, like you did last night? I'll get us a Chinese and all the kids and come back to yours ... try to get a bit of fun in our lives. What say you?"

"Thanks, that sounds a super idea," I whisper.

"Now hold it together and I'll see you at 6.30."

"I promise I'm out of tears now; honestly, there's not a drop left."

27

Karen

Monday 10.00am

I firmly believe that the following few days would have been a huge test for anyone. Your parents agree to move back in, to be with the girls whilst I keep vigil at Mum's bedside. Louise, bless her, is there for an hour daily, just to make sure that I eat, I guess. But where are you? Still upstairs in your hospital bed festering, completely self-absorbed. You could at least visit Mum, you could force yourself into a wheelchair and drag yourself downstairs, but instead you stay in your room and depress yourself even further. I'm not expecting sweetness and light from you but you could show your respects for Mum's sake. I'll never know what you're going through. I don't expect you to be a ray of sunshine but a tiny bit of support or love would go a long way.

Stroking Mum's tiny hand and talking gently is all I want to do. They say it could be anytime now, since they removed the drip, and yet she seems to be fighting, wanting to stay alive. That cuts me to the core as it makes me question whether I've made the right decision, but the nursing staff assure me that there is no alternative. To all intents and purposes, she is no longer there. How can this frail body have so much fight left?

I feel so alone lately. I'm permanently distraught and I've definitely aged in the last few months. My skin is grey and sallow, my hair is lifelessly tied tight in a ponytail. All that's left is to reminisce on the happy times, the years gone by, just the three of us—me, Mum and Dad. Memories are all I have. It's a constant strain. I can't think of our happy times as a family of four as that means I have to think of you and everything that has gone. It just makes me bitter.

Mum looks peaceful enough though; the enormous bruise on her face is fading daily, changing through various hues of the rainbow. The nursing staff remain incredible, offering me coffees, lunches, absolutely anything, they can't do enough. I recline in the large chair by Mum's bed and hold her hand, managing to nod off occasionally. The staff wake me periodically, so they can turn Mum gently and generally freshen her up.

When I feel like a break, I wander up to your ward, sit with you. I don't know why I bother, maybe it's a sense of duty. I know I'm torturing myself here though as you continue to be distant at best, plain nasty at worst. You are well aware of the extent of my dire situation but you're totally indifferent. You've lost interest in absolutely everything, especially where it concerns me. I'm furious with you at times. How you can be so completely heartless, right now of all times. I know it's all my fault. I feel your hatred towards me. Don't you think I'd like to turn the clock back as well?

I thought that telling you Jez had been arrested would make it better, but it seemed to make you worse. Now you're even more wired. I don't get it, there's just no pleasing you. Your progress is non-existent. Although your stump is healing well, the physio exercises are the only thing getting

176

you out of bed. Your depression has settled in nicely; the medical staff talk about referring you to a psychiatrist but you are adamant that you don't need it.

"There's nothing wrong with me. I just need to go home, back to my life, back to my work."

I am dreading you coming home. Life is bad enough at the moment, seeing you for one very long hour every day. I'm trying to fight with my feelings but the thought of you being back at home with us frightens the life out of me. The girls have noticed a marked change in their daddy too. Will we all adapt to our new life when you return?

After another exceptionally depressing long hour, I return downstairs to sit with Mum. Louise is there, my only spark of life. Even your parents are becoming tired with your moods lately.

"Come on, let's go for lunch. I'll tell the staff you're having a break."

"I don't know what I would do without you." I hug my best mate. "I owe you so, so much."

"Save it, let's go chill. They could do with a spa here, wouldn't you agree?"

She's crazy—but I love her.

Lunch is a real treat: tomato and basil soup, thick, warm crusty bread, jam sponge with custard for pudding, followed by a skinny decaff latté.

"That's the most I've seen you eat for weeks, hun."

"Yeah, I feel I need some carbs today, I've decided I'm going to get fat so Will won't want me back, so I'll just eat cake instead!"

Louise tries to maintain some normality by talking about projects for both of us which are in the pipeline, hopefully about two months away. In the past, we had produced a commercial for a sofa company in Manchester and they were looking to update it in August. We did an amazing job last time, so apparently the new project is earmarked for us.

"I can't think about any work at the moment. You understand, don't you."

"I know, just give yourself some space. Steve has helped us loads. He's always had a bit of a soft spot for you, hasn't he?" She winks as she says this.

"You're wicked!" Oh for those carefree days again. Steve was always teasing me. He always had us both laughing even when we were up against deadlines. He constantly told me I was like a five-year-old, twiddling with my hair. For a moment, memories of him make me smile.

"He's keeping things ticking over nicely. Let's face it, we are never exactly inundated with work, are we? It's not a problem, so don't worry."

As usual, she makes me laugh. Her kids have been amazing for Ellie and Jesse too. I don't know how I would have coped without them all.

All too soon it's time to go back upstairs to continue my vigil. Some *Hello!* and *OK!* magazines had been left by one of the nurses. I stay by Mum's side and the day crawls by.

At six o'clock I decide to go back home. I'm desperate to see the girls. Driving has become a blessing. Having been restricted, I've a new-found freedom being allowed to drive whilst my foot heals. I have stopped listening to the radio though, too many memories: either my parents or happier times with you.

The skin around my eyes feels dry, tight and swollen courtesy of the permanent stream of tears. They flow at any given moment and I've turned into a regular weeper, no matter where I am at the time. Either someone I pass in the shop resembles Mum, or there is a waft of Chanel no 5. No matter how random the event, it can reduce me to tears. My constant state of feeling torn between two worlds doesn't help. The minute I arrive home and hug the kids, all I want to do is to be back at Mum's bedside—there is no pleasing me.

This familiar routine happens every day for five days. Her breathing pattern has radically altered by day six. They tell me it is the next stage; it won't be long now.

You don't bother to visit until today; it is as though you have some sixth sense that she is about to go. I am gobsmacked when you wheel yourself in. You look dreadful, as always, and I can't deny that I am quite pleased that you appear totally guilt-ridden, with a constant frown on your face. You kiss me for the first time in weeks and stand on your good leg to kiss Mum, then you turn to face me.

"I'm sorry I've not been here for you. I know I'm being a complete arse, but I don't know what to do. I just can't snap myself out of it. It's not you, Karen, it's me. I'm in such a bad place."

It's the first couple of sentences from you in a long time. I want to reach out to you, to squeeze you tight, but I'm scared of further rejection. We both sit there and nothing else is said. There is nothing worth discussing in front of Mum. In a way, it is lovely: we just hold hands all afternoon. There is the odd interruption from the very sympathetic nursing staff, but generally it is silent.

Mum has started to make an unsettling rattling sound, a sure sign that the time is getting closer. We remain at her bedside for what seems like an eternity. Eventually you have to go back upstairs as your leg is playing up, so you leave me to take your painkillers. Maybe it's just an excuse to get away but at least you took the effort to come and for that I'm grateful.

I phone the girls to wish them both goodnight and speak briefly to your mum to say it isn't going to be long now. I want it all to happen quickly. Mum groans so I end the call immediately; it's as if she's in agony.

"You can go now," I whisper, gently kissing her soft cheek and brushing her hair. Silly things I find myself doing. I spray her favourite perfume on her long, thin hands. Tears stream. "I love you, Mum. I love you so much. You can go now, Dad is waiting."

Bizarrely, as if she needed my permission, Mum passes away within the next half hour. You return and are there for her last fifteen minutes.

"She has gone, babe."

The tears come. It's over. She looks so still and so peaceful and at last the dreadful noise has gone, leaving a deep chasm of silence. Her skin shiny, almost wax-like. She is gone: no breath, no movement, though she is still warm. I fall to the floor and sob, inconsolable and totally bereft. You buzz for a nurse. You don't have a clue what to do. We hug, but you are no longer my Will—he left me a long time ago.

The nurse enters discretely and at last you leave the room, phoning your parents as you wheel through the door. "Mary has passed away," I hear you say from the corridor.

The two staff nurses hug me; they couldn't be kinder.

"Go home, go get some sleep, come back tomorrow and we will talk about the next stages."

You leave me to go back to your room after one lifeless kiss, and I drive home. It's over; she's with Dad now. I am completely numbed and feel all alone in the world, no parents, I am an orphan.

Nothing much is said that night. Your parents are a comfort and they express their sorrow. It is unbelievable how much we have endured. They are both so concerned, for you and me, for us all. The string of events has taken its toll on each of us as well as on our marriage. Although they haven't seen us together recently, they are all too aware that there is a major problem looming, they're not stupid. There is nothing they can do, and they know it.

The twins are inconsolable when I try to explain that

their grandma has gone to heaven to be with Grandad. They've been through so much trauma these past few months, this seems the final straw for their fragile emotions. It has been a truly horrible year so far.

When your parents leave after putting the girls to bed, I pour myself a very large glass of wine and sit in complete silence, drained.

The next few days are a whirlwind of arrangements: flowers, coffins, priests, music, crematoriums, elegies and informing friends. There is no time to stand still and grieve, let alone function. I go into complete overdrive. Being an only child, it is all down to me. Your parents and Louise come into their own; they are beyond amazing. Even you manage to be relatively civil; you work very hard to put aside your own problems for the sake of us and the girls.

Finally, the day arrives. The weather provides an eerie low mist and the humidity is high—it's perfect funeral material. The thought of the event was far worse than attending it. Once the short, sweet ceremony is over, a ton of weight has lifted from my heavy shoulders. My only wish is that the whole thing had lasted longer, all day perhaps. It seemed to be over in moments for someone who had lived for so long. The support from close friends and family is overwhelming. The most beautiful sympathy cards, flowers, texts and phone calls. I realise just how many good friends we have, and how special they have become to me and the girls.

The wake is pleasant, with many exchanging stories, old school friends reminiscing about how they had all adored mum; she had been quite a cool mother in her day. The twins find it amusing to hear of the antics their granny had got up to years ago, when I was their age.

You remain distant. It's obvious and it's embarrassing. It's the first time most of these people have seen you struggling in your wheelchair with one leg. I guess neither you or they know what to say.

28

Karen

Wednesday 10.15am, three days later

Three days following Mum's funeral and the time feels
right to clear out my parents' home. I guessed you wouldn't
exactly miss me for a couple of days, so I treat myself to
a large Starbucks and drive out on the familiar route. The
thirty-minute drive seems to take moments.

When I arrive I'm in a daze—so much has gone on,
so much to take in. Thanks to the cleaning company, the
apartment is immaculate. I take a few of Mum's favourite
lavender candles and light one in each room to remind me
of her. This apartment still seems new to me. They were
only in their late fifties when they decided to downsize—
way too young, in my opinion. This place is so different
to the enormous three-bedroom Georgian house I grew
up in. It was a sad day the day they decided to downsize,
but still they managed release some equity and have fun.
I'm glad they did it now, in hindsight. Buying this place
gave them a new spark in their life, a bit of freedom. No

large garden to maintain, no large house to clean, they had more money for holidays and more time to spend with us. Clearing this is going to be a mammoth task without you. Still, it's a good excuse to have some peace. I don't feel a bit guilty being here. I'm mourning and I think it will do you some good to be without me for a few days.

I sip my coffee and have a wander around. "OK, I give myself three days then I'll get the clearance company in," I promise myself out loud. "Now, where shall I begin? The lounge is as good a place as any." The last time I was here, it was all too emotional. Now it's a comfort to be here.

Looking around, I thank God once more that they did downsize. If I'd had to clear the old house it could have taken months, so for that I'm grateful.

The lounge is the obvious place to start and within five minutes I am drifting. I shake myself and tell myself to get on with it. I decide to tackle the large display cabinet which stretches across a whole wall first. There's a couple of photo albums which go straight into one of the white plastic boxes I've brought with me, no distractions. I'll go through those later with the girls. I can't bring myself to look at them right now, and we can always frame our favourites if we take time to look at them another day. If three days is my target, then I can't afford to get side-tracked. Any paperwork will go straight into a separate white box marked urgent.

One small tin in a drawer has obviously not been opened for a while and I have to prize it open with a knife. Inside, tightly packed, is a roll of ten pound notes. "Oh my God!" It's £350 to be exact. Poor thing, she had become so confused. There is no clear explanation as why she would stash so much money in a small tin. "Handbag, where is it?" I'd been talking to myself all day. "OK, I'll put that away, somewhere safe."

In the third drawer is a small square wallet. "Oh blimey!" I'd bought this twenty-five years ago from a tiny gift shop in Nerja, Spain. That was the only time I'd gone into the town and left the pool because it had been roasting that week. Little Mermaid, they called me. "Mum, you're an old devil." The purse is red leather with two gold flamenco dancers embossed on the front, a typical Spanish wallet. Our girls will love that. Again, inside, another roll—this time a mixture of £10 and £20 pound notes — £430 in total. I lean back on my heels, speechless in astonishment for a moment. "I hope you can both see me. Why didn't you bloody spend this?"

I pull the drawer out completely, just to check to see if anything had gone down the back. Now, knowing what Mum was like, I will have to be vigilant and check the most obscure of places.

I eye up the settee as I stand up, put my hands on my hips and think, *OK, Mum, let's see if you have hidden any more money.* Sure enough, under the seat cushions of the settee and each armchair are three small boxes. "What's she like?" I laugh. Using the knife to prize the lids (these boxes do not open very easily), I find in each tin, as before, a roll of money: £200, £275, £460. Every time I count, I can hear either Mum or Dad: "Go spend it on the kids, love, buy them something nice with it."

One thing I desperately want to find is Mum's old jewellery box. I am wearing her wedding ring given to me by the nursing staff, but somewhere in this apartment is the jewellery box that I used to play with. Within the TV cabinet are three drawers: the top one is bursting full of wires which spill out as I try to wrench it open. I give it a hefty tug and spy a collection of TV remotes and a small bundle of letters tied together with an elastic band. The first one has 'Dearest Karen' written on the front in Dad's handwriting. I gasp and tears burn the back of my eyes. "I can't open it ... I can't read it just yet."

The rest of the drawer is emptied: guarantees, instructions and plugs and an odd couple of small keys.

"OK, I wonder what you guys are for?" I put them in my jeans pocket. I place the envelope on the settee. "I'll get the bedroom done next," I promise myself. "I'll leave the envelope till I have my next coffee break." I say it as if they are both there beside me in the room.

The bed has been stripped. "I'll just check under the mattress." Oh God, this time an envelope with nothing written on it. I open it to find yet another wedge of notes: £1500. My hands shake. "Mum ... Dad!" I shout this time, "I told you to go on that cruise, you should have treated yourselves!"

"I never spend the bloody money," I can hear Mum say.

"Treat yourself, go spend." That was Dad's voice.

In the bedroom cupboard behind a mountain of shoes is the old money box I always wanted to get my hands on as a child—it's locked, but there is definitely something in it. The two keys in my pocket won't open it. It's a fair old weight and it jingles as though full of coins, lots of them. "Right, you can go in a white box, and we'll see if Louise can open you for me later, she's a dab hand with tools! Next!"

At the back of the cupboard is my old jewellery box; in it are eight odd gold stud earrings. I was always losing one of a pair—still do, in fact. There are also a few broken gold bangles, three boxed link gold bracelets, and my gold watch given to me by my parents when I was eighteen. "Bloody hell, I thought I'd lost that, but I was too scared to tell you, Mum." All these things are placed carefully into a white plastic box. "Three more drawers left then I'm having that coffee." The envelope in the lounge is at the back of my mind and gives me the incentive to push on. I want to enjoy reading it at my leisure.

In one of Dad's old jackets is his wallet with £30 pounds in it; the old threadbare wallet almost smelled of him. Mum's purse will be an interesting one, she always had us searching high and low for it. *Has to be in one of her handbags*, I thought.

"OK, coffee time!" I'm shattered and drag myself up onto my feet and head towards the kitchen.

The kettle needs a clean so I empty the old water, give it a rinse and fill it with new. My old Easter egg mug is still in the cupboard—Kit Kat. I'll keep this one. The coffee has solidified in the tin so I have to chip away at it with a knife. The sugar jar always made me laugh; none of us had taken sugar for years, but Mum would still ask, "How many sugars?" *I wonder*, and sure enough, another hiding place for £825. This is becoming silly now! I can hear them both having a good laugh every time I find a new stash. Mum must have set this up over the past couple years, or was this part of her disease, leaving things in confused places? Ah, poor old thing. Either way, today has turned out to an amusing day. The tea caddy is full of teabags. However, the biscuit tin is, yet again, filled with notes, all scrunched up, this time as if placed in a hurry. "Oh, bless her." It amounts to a further £475. At this rate, I'm going to need a Securicor van to get home!

I sit in the lounge and read.

Hey gorgeous girl,

Dad always called me this. I take a deep breath, hold it, and continue reading.

I don't know the circumstances in which you will be reading this letter. I will have gone by now but if Mum is still alive then I hope you are with her. Her memory has been shocking for the past few years. I have been trying to cover for her, but I think she might have Alzheimer's or dementia. Her mother had dementia and ended up in a home, years ago, before you were born. I never wanted to say anything about Mum because it's such a cruel, misunderstood disease. I didn't want her to know

187

anything was wrong. Maybe you already know, maybe she is gone too by the time you read this. Anyway, I am rambling.

We never said much to you over the years, but we wanted to tell you how very proud we are. We are both so proud of you and your achievements, but moreover the person you have become. You are the light in our lives, little Miss Sunshine, and always the apple of our eye. We now see it in your two beautiful girls. They have the amazing ability of lighting up any room they enter, just like you. Your job always made us laugh; we never quite understood exactly what it was you did for a living. It didn't stop us admiring you. One thing we know is that you have done extremely well in your career. All your Mum and I ever wished for was that you would be happy and would have a lovely family life, so that you could understand how much we adored you. You have all that and more. Will is a superb choice of partner for you. We wanted to wish you all the very best for your future, and being hopeless with words, we thought by writing you this letter we could say all the mushy stuff without you laughing at us old codgers.

Don't ever change, sweetheart. We know that all the decisions you have to make in your life will be well considered, honest and kind choices. We wish we could be with you all the way through your life, but you know that is not possible. Let me and your mum stay in your heart forever. We love you so much. You will never know just how much. Take care and enjoy every moment, live every day like your last.

One more thing before I sign off. Beware the tins in the apartment, honey. I hid Mum's things because I didn't want her to lose them, with her terrible memory. You'll understand. Enjoy the treasure hunt.

Love you, my sweetheart,

Dad and Mum
xxxxxxxxxx

"I think I am going to frame this, Dad, and put it somewhere I can see it every day." Kissing the paper, I fold it carefully and place it in the white box with all the photos. "So you have given me a little treasure hunt, have you, you old devils?" I look around and have a good laugh. "I think I've had enough excitement for one day." With that, I grab my bag, gather up the full boxes, lock up and leave.

My evening is spent at the hospital, trying to talk to you, trying to tell you all about my day. I don't know why I bother. You just glare at me, looking right through me. The warmth you demonstrated when Mum was passing is long gone and you continue to be in your own world. You would have thought that with our financial situation in its present state that you would find some form of comfort with today's results from my treasure hunt; however, the news falls on deaf ears, you couldn't give a damn! I kiss your forehead and I am gone.

Back home, the girls are having a great time with Louise and her kids. McDonald's chicken nuggets, chips and a McFlurry are waiting for me. As much as I hate fast food, this time it is eaten with relish whilst I tell Louise all about my unexpected day.

"Looks like my dad hid quite a lot of the money. He did have a wicked sense of humour, I bet he loved planting tins and envelopes here, there and everywhere."

"Lucky you! Sounds like a top day. At last something lovely has happened."

"He also left me a really sweet letter, which was not like him. He wasn't good at soppy stuff. I'm going to frame it."

"Now, that's a brilliant idea. Love it!"

"They weren't the sort of parents to tell me how much they loved me. That's probably why I tell mine each day how proud I am of them, how much they are loved. It is so great to have that letter there, in black and white, something to keep forever. I miss them both so much."

The kids are all quietly sat watching Wallace and Gromit's *The Wrong Trousers*, one of our favourites.

"Wine?"

"Yeah, just one. I have to drive home, you know."

"I need to stop this; it's becoming a bad habit just lately. Everyone keeps feeding me white wine. I'm going to be a regular at Alcoholics Anonymous at this rate." I grab the neck of yesterday's Chablis from the fridge, pull out the cork and pour the remaining half bottle into two large glasses.

"Listen to me. With the crap you've been through this year, I'd be on heroin by now! All in moderation, eh! Cheers, hun." Louise raises her glass and we chink together. We'll sort out your forthcoming alcohol problem when life has settled down a bit. Deal?"

"Deal. Cheers to friendship!"

Day two at the apartment. I stand at the door, wondering where to start. "OK, so what am I going to find here today then?" I decide to begin with the little job that Mum was always going to do—take Dad's things to the charity shop. She never could get to grips with throwing away his clothes. I rifle through Dad's coat pockets, not that surprised by now to find more money. Not stashes as before, but the odd £50 here, £80 there. "Before I die, I am going to do exactly the same for our girls, I promise. Thanks, Dad."

Under the mattress, true to form, another envelope, this time with a huge 'X' on the front. Inside is £1000. It takes my breath away. I knew it was going to be full of money, but not as much as this! The drawers are full of the usual items. I pull out the bottom one to make sure nothing had slipped to the back. An old glasses case with a taped-up pair of ready readers slightly conceals a bundle of twenties beneath it, another £500. On the left of an old wallet is a photo of the three of us in better days. *What a handsome couple they were and how happy, about the same age as me and you... How they looked so in love, not like us!* "I think today is going to be another emotional one!" I say to the room.

There is an old briefcase I used to play doctors with, aged about four, at the bottom of the wardrobe. It's standing proud as if to say 'Time to find more treasure.' Something heavy is in it, but it's locked. I remember the keys in my trouser pocket from yesterday, and suspect it could be the one to open it. "I'll open it later," I mutter.

The kitchen was always going to be the mother of all jobs: pots, pans, plates, the usual. The food cupboard is rammed to capacity with twenty tins of soup, ten tins of beans, twenty tins of peas, jars of jam and marmalade, tins of tuna, all stashed away as if war was imminent. This can all go to the clearance team and maybe the food bank. The mop cupboard is hilarious. Poor mum, being so confused, had stockpiled at least thirty toilet rolls, seven bleaches, five large boxes of washing powder and other essentials, all crammed in. Looks like every time Mum went out, she would top up the same things, but never actually use them. Her handbags were in there too—no wonder she could never find them — and another set of keys.

In one of her bags is Mum's gold watch; it was Dad's present to her for their thirty-fifth wedding anniversary. I distinctly remember her getting upset when it went missing a while ago. She was convinced someone had stolen it, but looks like it was here all the time. There's a pair of heart-shaped diamond earrings here too with the watch, nothing too flash, but very pretty nevertheless. In the same handbag is the purse, and inside another £100 of notes and some loose change. The notes look fresh from the bank. There in the very back of the cupboard is the jewellery box. This is something to save till I get home. The white boxes are filling up nicely, and I am getting through the apartment a lot quicker than yesterday.

The dining room appears to have been unused for years, with everything perfectly in its place. Mum hasn't eaten in here for some time. The room looks like an easy one to sort, only containing a wall unit displaying crystal glasses and vases, and two pictures hanging on the wall. I wrap each glass, vase and the decanter with care. Mum had treasured her crystal and, as much as I dislike it, it is sacrilege to give it away. Once the cupboards are carefully emptied, it is time for the drawers. The top drawer contains posh knives and forks and a small tin with a heart on top—£100. The second drawer: tablemats, another tin (this time with a kiss on it, £200). The third drawer has a smiley face on it and contains £300. Drawer number four holds napkins and a tin with two hearts on it—£400.

With a very heavy heart, I have to wrench myself away as it is time to collect our twins from school. I haven't had to do that in a few weeks, thanks to my very incredible network of friends. But I perk myself up as I realise I can't wait to hear their excited chatter, to hear what they've been up to today. It'll be refreshing to be on the playground again meeting the mums.

They make a huge fuss of me. It's been a long time.

Day three, time for the shed. Scruffs on today as this one is going to be messy. Not the most enthralling of jobs, and I am not looking forward to it. Dad had always been a keen gardener in the early days, but when they downsized they ended up with a cute little courtyard and a small shed at the back. Inside are various gardening tools, strimmer and a tiny work area with hammers, saws, screwdrivers and a collection of screws and nails. Cobwebs and all sorts of bugs have collected in all the nooks and crannies. This is not the nicest of jobs, and once again I wish you were here with me. I decide to work rapidly as I am feeling grubbier by the minute. The only bonus is that the shed is not very large, so hopefully this isn't going to take too long.

I don't know if you remember, but Dad served in the Royal Navy and travelled all over in his youth, so the shed is full of old relics from Gibraltar, Brazil and various other naval bases dotted around the world. On the back wall is a leather case that looks like it holds a rifle. Opening it carefully, I discover it's Dad's old Navy sword. "Wow! Oh my God! This is beautiful!" It takes me back, admiring the beautiful engravings down the length of the silver blade. It's in immaculate condition. Typical of Dad, the leather case looks untouched, as does the rich golden handle. I remember it now, but haven't seen it for a good twenty years. Underneath it is a black steel box covered in dust. Taking the sword and the box, that is the shed finished. It's time to lock up and go back home.

Louise is at ours again; she's practically moved in.

"Hi honey, I'm home!" We laugh. "I feel like I'm married to you these days."

"With respect, is that wishful thinking?"

"Ha, love that saying! *With respect*—it always means that something profoundly disrespectful is going to be said."

"How did day three of the treasure hunt go?"

"Well, maybe you can help me; I have two boxes that I need to get into, and one briefcase that I think I have a key for."

"How exciting! Hand them over. I always loved your parents, they were so cool."

Louise gets stuck in whilst I grab a quick shower, washing my grubby day away.

I take a sneaky peek at the kids in the lounge, all four huddled together on the settee watching TV.

"It's like a bloody crèche in that lounge! Would you like a glass of cava? I feel a celebration coming on." I ask as I walk back into the kitchen, feeling much brighter.

"Great! I've ordered us all a Chinese for 7 o'clock.

Thought you've probably built up an appetite."

"Fabulous! How you getting on?"

"Need a screwdriver. Do you have one?"

I go to the garage and raid some tools from your toolbox.

"How's this?" I laugh, brandishing a screwdriver. It's never been touched. "I bought him this for Christmas. He loves tools; it's a man thing I guess."

"Looks like we can do some damage with that."

I now wave a chisel in one hand and a brand-new hammer in the other. "Looks like Will's clearly never used these items before."

The black steel box from the shed is the first to be opened. Inside are some beautiful medals from his Navy days, still in their presentation boxes.

"Oh God, these are beautiful! They are so precious! Why didn't he ever have them on display?"

"He was always very modest about his time in the forces. I found his sword today, and I'm going to hang it on the wall in the hallway. It might stop anymore intruders. It's stunning!"

"Proper treasure hunt today, then!"

"Yes, well and truly. I think it's all done now, though. Got the clearance company going in tomorrow and the estate agent going in on Monday. I want things to be sorted as soon as possible. Too many things are going on for me at the moment."

"Don't blame you; I think I would do exactly the same in your shoes."

"OK, the jewellery box next. I'll have a look at that. Do you think you can get this money box open?"

"Pass me the tools and I'll do my damndest."

"Ha, this is great fun. Just so typical of my dad, isn't it!"

"Sure is. I wonder if your mum was in on it before she got sick."

"We'll never know. I'd like to think she was. It gives me

some form of comfort."

As the money box is jimmied opened, coins splay out everywhere across the floor, prompting the kids to pile in.

"What's all the noise, Mum? What's happening?"

"Well, give us a minute and let's see. I found this at Nanny and Grandad's flat. OK, you lot—" I turn to the kids "—can you count this for me?"

"Woooow!" they say in unison.

"That should keep you all quiet for a bit." I empty another tray of coins on the floor and the kids get stuck in. "There you go, there's more."

They are so excited it makes us both laugh.

"Nanny and Grandad must have been rich, eh?" Little Ellie nudges me as she says it. Sometimes she can be so grown up.

"Looks like it, get counting."

Underneath both trays are three huge rolls of money. Louise and I just stare at each other. Beneath the money is a piece of paper with a big smiley face on it.

"He must have had so much fun planting all this around the place."

"It's his gift to you. What a wonderful thing to do!"

Three thousand pounds are counted in notes; the kids count £325 in coins.

"I love Grandad," says Jesse, as the kids dance around the kitchen.

The jewellery box is full of expensive and unusual jewels, some I've never seen. I am mesmerised. Louise and I chink our glasses and do a toast to my parents.

"This is going down in one." I grin, pouring myself another one.

"Not for me, I'm driving."

"Stay the night, all of you, then we can celebrate."

"Can we, Mum, can we?" Louise's kids are going crazy.

"Go on then, fill my glass up." She hands me her flute.

The briefcase stored fifteen thousand pounds' worth of premium bonds. Dumbfounded, we both stare at the paperwork, then scream and pour ourselves another glass.

The doorbell rings.

"Chinese, yeah!" The kids jump up and race to the door.

The takeaway's amazing, and it is the best night me and my girls have experienced since before the attack. The kids stay up till 11pm and Louise and I go to bed finally at about oneish.

"We are going to be so ill in the morning." Louise runs her hands through her hair.

"Yep, we sure are, but I've enjoyed every minute of this. It's the first time in ages that I feel normal."

29

Friday

But the good times had to come to an end, of course they did.

Why did you not sit down and explain how unbearable your life has become? How you feel? How you're totally consumed with hate? You hate Jez. You hate life. You hate your disability and you hate being anywhere near me. Instead, daily you torment yourself, you mutter. I hear you, constantly criticising and complaining that nothing is good enough.

When you finally come home, things only become worse. There's no doctors or nurses to act up in front of here, so me and the girls face your permanent foul tempers, sarcastic quips and general nastiness. It's a sad atmosphere to be living in. Take it out on me by all means, but not the girls. You insist on sleeping downstairs as well, to be as far away as possible from me. I'm happy with that arrangement too, for the time being at least, but I'm not giving up on you just yet.

I heard you this afternoon: "I'm so fucking stupid, should have kept my mouth shut."

God knows what you meant by that.

"If only she hadn't booked the bloody charity ball, the stupid log cabin. Why didn't we stay in that Friday night?"

Yep hun, I've asked myself the same questions many times. Of course, it's all my fault!

"How come she's picking up? I don't see her suffering. She acts like nothing's happened. Her pathetic little injury is merely a scratch, doesn't give her any pain or any grief." Another chant under your breath is, "Everyone loves Karen: happy, smiley, sickly Karen."

You think no one hears you. It upset me to start with but I'm just seeing your true colours now, I guess. You can't bear to look at me. Mind you, I've become used to that too. You want your old life back, as simple as that, but it's eating at you, every single minute of every single day. Your life and your wife are driving you insane. Counselling, everyone keeps saying have counselling, but you don't need to explain how you feel to any shrink, you know exactly how you feel. You hate me, you hate your life, and you hate yourself even more. Business is going down the pan rapidly, money is non-existent, it's a total mess. The only blessing we have is from my parents' treasure hunt. I still need a spare half hour to tally up how much it all comes to.

In my darkest days, I've asked myself if I can live without you. I'd ask for a divorce but the sadistic side of me has persuaded myself to carry on. I'm hanging on for any spark in my life I can find. But it's not happening though, is it? The more I try, the more you push me away. It's a no-win situation.

Your parents invite us to their house in Wales, not too far for you to sit in the car. It's a perfect idea. They're concerned too, so they think it would be a good thing to get away, get us out of the house, to have bit of a break. Our little family hasn't been anywhere since May. We all need space, a change of scene, and you more than any of us. Me and the girls have responded well to the counselling, thanks to Louise's friend, but you don't need help, do you?

The night before, you and I sit together. I have a glass of wine and you are on your fourth large whiskey. I try to coax some form of conversation out of you, try to get you to open up to me. Finally, you break down.

"Hun, I know I've been a complete tosser to live with. I can't help myself. I'm so angry; I'm angry all the time. I'm finding it really hard to, or like anything at the moment, like I'm under a dark cloud. Maybe this weekend we can try to get some quality time, whatever the hell that means anymore, but I just feel like we'll never get back to how we were. I'm not sure I even want to be anymore. I'm no good here, babe. I'm dragging you down. There's no pleasing me. I don't know what I want. I'm just so flat."

The last time I saw you in bits like this was when you were told of your amputation. You're shaking in my arms and you're not letting me go. I feel like we are getting somewhere, a conversation, a breakthrough, for these moments at least. Can we make it together? Is there an iota of hope? I hope so.

The day for our escape to Wales dawns with glorious sunshine, not a cloud in the sky—quite a change from the early low mist that seems to have plagued us the last few weeks. I know you didn't sleep last night. I know you haven't had a proper night's sleep in months. Nightmares, anxiety, stress, hate and fear—it's all kept you awake. Sometimes you've screamed out loud—night terrors, I suppose. I hear you downstairs. I know you have a few more whiskeys (I've started to measure the bottles when you're not around). I hear you muttering to yourself; I watch you, I sit on the stairs. You can't see me though, it seems like you are there for hours, with your alcohol and painkillers—your new best friends, the only things you can depend on. With the lack of food intake, it is all beginning to show. You've lost so much weight. OK, you've always looked athletic, and in the past you could eat cakes all day yet still not gain weight, but now you're gaunt, older looking and painfully thin. It shows in your yellow, almost jaundiced face, which makes your hollow bloodshot eyes stand out even more. The hangovers only increase your moods and you've started to develop a slight twitch, particularly first thing. I'm no doctor but I know you are one hundred percent depressed and it looks like it's not going away anytime soon.

We pack the car up in record time. It is the first time I've seen the girls laugh properly in ages and it even brings a smile to my face. They squeeze into the back seat, surrounded by pillows, sleeping bags and tablets loaded with cartoons. I'm about to get into the driving seat when you announce that you're not coming. You apparently want some space. I sigh in resignation. You're unbelievable! Maybe you can't bring yourself to even be in the same car as me, let alone have a weekend away. You don't say that but I'm not stupid. To be honest, I have all but given up on you, despite last night, and I'm glad to have time without you being continually aggressive and feeling sorry for yourself, pushing us all away. Your self-pity is infuriating. Perhaps last night was just the alcohol talking. I bet you don't even remember a word of it.

I turn to leave but you grab my arm and give me a long, passionate hug, almost like the old days. The girls realise that something is wrong and have jumped out of the car to join us in the embrace.

"Love you all, be safe, drive carefully," you say, and I notice there's tears in your eyes. You look like you care.

It takes us just over thirty minutes to get there. The traffic isn't too bad, although we did get stuck behind an extremely slow tractor. The girls are so excited, still a bit clingy with me but I'm not complaining. Out of the four of us, I think Jesse and Ellie have progressed the most and are doing well, but there is still a lot of healing that needs to take place. The counselling sessions have proved to be amazing. There's fewer nightmares and at last things are finally moving in the right direction at least for them.

When we finally arrive, your parents are clearly upset that you're not with us. Like me, they had hoped that you would at least try. It's not happening though, is it? Not for the moment anyway. It is going to take you a lot more time.

Your mum has prepared the most amazing afternoon tea for us all and the conservatory is the ideal venue. The sweet smell of cakes and flowers hits us as we enter the room. The table has been set with paper party napkins, jelly babies dotted around the tablecloth and an enormous vase of pink roses provides a fragrant centrepiece. I feel as though we are in an exclusive restaurant in the countryside. The patio doors open onto their vast perfectly manicured garden, and it is so lovely to be surrounded by fresh air. What an ideal place you were bought up in!

Your mum's a far better cook than my mum ever was and she's prepared all our favourites: the lightest lemon drizzle cakes that practically melt in your mouth, and her scones are in a class of their own. Even her sandwiches are made to perfection, with crusts professionally removed, just how we all like them. It's an absolute treat! It is all washed down with a crisp glass of champagne for the adults and her homemade lemonade for the girls. It doesn't take away how sad they feel with you not being here, or lessen our concern. I don't admit it to them, that I am actually glad. Your absence has made me feel guilty, but I don't miss the constant daggers and the way you look directly through me. Life has not been good. Still, even though you probably can't remember last night, I think there was some evidence that you still love me, a nanosecond of hope?

Maybe you're right though, a weekend on your own might just do you some good.

"Nanny, I love these baby sandwiches, they are so cute," mumbles little Jesse through a mouthful of cheese and ham.

"Mmmm yummy!" Ellie makes us all laugh because she has so much in her mouth she's unable to speak.

We all tuck into the lemon drizzle cakes then the scones, jam and cream. It is pure indulgence. After tea, the girls are straight out into the garden where they play for hours with the balloons, presents from Granny and Grandpops. Your parents insist we sit in the living room and tidy away later. I love the Chesterfields in here, it's a total contrast to the conservatory, so much cosier. I'm expecting a waiter to turn up any moment and serve us all. Your parents have spoiled us rotten and I have no desire to go back home. There's more champagne to finish off and we are all so full it's hard to move. For the first time in months I'm chilling. There's a mountain of magazines your mum and I sift through and your dad is content with his newspaper. It's been ages since I've been so relaxed. I feel things could possibly be headed in the right direction: our conversation last night, your warm hug this morning and now I'm wishing you had come with us. I think this would've done you the world of good. Every now and then we stop to laugh at the twins giggling uncontrollably in the garden. They're so loud today and it's great to hear them both have fun at last.

Before we know it, an hour and a half has passed, your dad has just woken up from a snooze and your mum and I have finished flicking through the magazines. It's time to clear away. As we start taking things to the kitchen, the conversation starts. Your parents have been very polite not to ask, but they're obviously full of questions.

"How is he? Why didn't come? We are so worried, love!" Your poor dad, I've not seen him so close to tears.

"He said he wanted some space. He's been so hard to be around. I'm sorry, but I wasn't going to argue with him. We were all so excited to come and see you, I wasn't going to let Will ruin it."

"No, you did the right thing, sweetheart," your mum agrees whilst packing away the empty plates.

"Maybe it's a blessing. It might do him some good. He's been surrounded by people for months now. Perhaps being on his own might make him think about the future. Take stock, as they say. He'll be fine on his own, he might even miss you and the kids." Your dad places the chairs back under the table, trying to make himself busy.

"Thanks for your understanding. You've been so good to us. When we really needed you, you were there. I cannot thank you enough." My eyes fill up by I'm determined not to cry.

"Don't worry, love; it's a real comfort to see you and the girls." She gives me one of her hugs which makes me miss my mum all the more.

"That was such an amazing tea. You know, you should think about going into business."

"Ah, you're a love."

"No, I mean it. That was amazing!"

She folds the tea towel, placing it carefully on the worktop. "How's he getting on with his prosthetic?"

"Not very well. It gives him blisters, so he only wears it when the physio comes. He's not progressing at all. He's aggressive to me and he rarely speaks to the girls. Even they've mentioned it. He hates me. I think he blames me for everything. He permanently looks guilt-ridden, but I'm the one that should be guilty, I bid for the stupid log cabin."

"I'm sure that's not true, Karen."

"No, it is. He just gives me yes/no answers all the time. He's a regular Jekyll and Hyde. If anyone comes to the house, he's amazing with them. He's amazing with everyone except me and in the past week, as I say, he's even been off with the twins. I can't reach out to him. He's refusing to go to counselling; he insists he doesn't need it. Our lady counsellor is amazing; she comes to the house and she's been brilliant! I did get a little glimmer of hope from Will last night though and today. When we left he even hugged me. He was lovely this morning, so you never know."

It's still light outside and the girls are playing on your old tree swing. They're so hilarious to watch we decide to stay in the conservatory, as we can see them better.

As if you can sense what I'm saying, my mobile bleeps a text from you.

```
I love you babe. I know I'm a mess,
but I really do love you. Say hi for
me. Tell them I love them too. I'm
going to try to get some sleep. Love
you, babe. x
```

I'm silent for a while, re-reading your text again and again.

```
You   too   hun.   See   you   tomorrow
xxx
```

I reply.

Showing my phone to your parents, still not quite believing the warmth of your text, I blink back tears.

"I think he means this. It's the first lovely thing he has said in ... since before..." My voice trails off. "I don't know how long ... except for last night. Maybe he is turning a corner, maybe when I go home tomorrow night he'll be a changed man, or at least a step in the right direction."

The awkward silence is broken by your dad.

"Anyway, let's just enjoy our time together, for the

sake of the girls. Cheers. Let's relax, ladies, and enjoy the weekend!" Your dad is so sweet; he always knows what to say.

We drink another glass each, which empties the bottle, as we watch Ellie and Jesse lark around in the garden. They are always good entertainment, and we've always said no television is needed when our twins are around.

It is so lovely to chill out in Wales, but we all miss you. The weather is forecast to be glorious, and it doesn't disappoint. Your dad and I go for a stroll down the lane to try to walk off some of the cakes. It's leafy and green and we even see the occasional wild poppy. The trees rustle with the welcomed breeze. It's almost a relief to be in the shade from the afternoon sun.

"It's so peaceful here, you really are in the middle of nowhere. It's wonderful!"

"We love it. Maybe one day you and Will might live here when we're long gone."

"That's an awfully long time away, why don't we just move in now?" I tease.

"Now there's an idea!"

I am thoroughly enjoying myself. I feel so free. As if your mum hasn't done enough for us, she's prepared your favourite—chicken and chorizo casserole—for tea, after which we all collapse to watch *Chicken Run* on the TV.

The girls go to bed just before ten, exhausted. Your mum had bought them both some *Frozen* pyjamas so they happily give us a fashion show before saying goodnight. I follow them up to tuck them in. It's been a long, fun day and they are both asleep within minutes.

My foot is still giving me a bit of trouble in the evenings, so I unpack my bag and dig around in my toiletry bag for some pain relief. That's when I find your note. It's written on a ripped piece of notepaper folded into the side pocket. It's your handwriting but I can tell you were either drinking or in a hurry when you wrote it as it's not as neat as usual. You always had beautiful writing. I sit before I read it because in the past few months it's the last thing I expect from you.

Hi Babe,
I honestly don't know where to begin. I love you so much. I just can't show it anymore. I don't know how to be me.
It's not your fault what happened in the log cabin that night, it was mine. It was all my stupid fault.

You know the night of the charity ball, well I bumped into Jez.

"What?"

Well, in fact, he came up to me, offered to light my cigar. I think you were in the loo at the time. I was outside. He completely threw me. I didn't know what to say. He frightened me a bit to be honest.

I struggle for breath. "Oh my God!" I whisper with my hand firmly over my mouth.

I didn't recognise him at first. He looked so old. I tried to get away but he grabbed my wrist and told me I owed him one. He rambled on about Jeanie. I wasn't listening, my head was all over the place. He wrote his phone number on a scrap piece of paper and told me to phone him. He threatened me. He told me he knew people, cons that would harm us both if I didn't get in contact with him.

My heart is in my throat. It's difficult to read. I'm fuming. Disbelief, total disbelief. You let me believe it was *all my fault*.

The showroom (as you've since found out, thanks to Lois, she shouldn't have told you) has been spiralling for the past eighteen months. I was going to go under, I needed some cash. He gave me an idea — maybe if he burgled us we could claim it back, put the money back into the business. So, three long days after the charity do, I was at work staring at his number.

He was just supposed to burgle us, to steal the car. He'd get your jewellery and we'd claim on the house insurance, but the prick went too far, didn't he!

I cannot believe what I am reading.

Clearly he wanted revenge and I fell for it like a plonker. I can't believe I was so stupid.

All this time I thought you blamed me. All this time, you made *me* feel guilty. You've been so damn nasty towards me, yet all this time *you* and *Jez* planned to attack us. Attack me and our kids, *your own kids*, to save *your precious* business.

Now look at us! I'm helpless. I can't work, I can't function, I can't love. But I do love you, I never stopped loving you. But I can't get through this. By the time you read this I will be gone. I'm going to make it look like an accident, so you cannot show this letter to anyone. I love you so much but I can't do this anymore. Please make me happy and just find someone else. You deserve to be happy, you and our girls. Please don't let them hate me. I love them and Mum and Dad too. You mustn't show this letter to anyone. I don't want you to lose the house. You need to get the life insurance. Please, babe, promise to do this for me. Please don't hate me. I want this. I can't do this life anymore.

I Love you so, so much.

"Will, baby, no…"

The note slips from my hand as I attempt to stand, but I'm frozen, not knowing where to start, what to do. I feel sick. What have you done? I grab the note and charge down to the lounge to your parents, who are still watching the TV.

"What, Karen? What is it, love?" Your dad leaps to his feet. Instinctively he knows something is wrong.

I force the note into your dad's hand, not trusting myself to speak, the words won't come.

Eventually I stutter, "We must…" I struggle to breathe "…stop him. Please, please, he can't…"

"What, love?" your mum coaxes me, moving towards me, then realisation strikes and her hand covers her mouth.

"He set it up!"

"What, Karen? What do you mean?" Your dad looks at me in confusion.

"He met up with Jez. He set the whole thing up. He knew we were going to be burgled."

"No Karen, you're wrong!"

"Our Will wouldn't do a thing like that!" Your mum sits hard in the chair, her hands covering her face.

"Read it!" I tear the note from your dad's grasp and shove it into her hands.

"We've got to go before he does something stupid!" I sob in a rush.

"Karen, love, get your keys."

"I'll stay here with the girls. They can't see their dad like…" Your mum can't find the words to finish her sentence.

30

Saturday night 10pm

Your dad reads the note, his hands shaking. "No, son, no!" Your mum is in bits, tears streaming down her face.

"Karen, get your things, quick, we are going there now!" Your dad's fists are clamped to his side, trying to control himself and the situation. He places his hands on your mum's shoulders. "I'll sort him, love. Are you OK here?"

"Yes, you two go. I'll stay with the kids. They don't need to see … this." She's stuck for words, your poor mum.

I rush to get my things: keys, phone, bag. *Please let us not be too late.*

It's a race to get to you, and your dad is driving like a man possessed. The lanes are black and winding, no one else on them, thank God. He swerves several times, once to avoid a large badger wandering across the road with not a care in the world, unlike us. We're desperate to get to you.

Your poor dad keeps banging the steering wheel, tears streaming down his cheeks, driving way over the speed limit. I try the police with your dad's phone, our house with my phone. I try your mobile, but there's no signal from either of our phones. We've hit a mobile dead zone. I dial again. Still no signal, nothing.

"Jesus, I can't get through. What are we going to do?" I scream.

The rural lanes take me back to that night in the car with Jez, the cause of all this. As if in some sort of muscle memory, my foot starts to throb.

Your dad takes a deep breath, his knuckles white on the steering wheel. "OK, Karen, let's both try to be calm. When we get a signal, I'll stop the car and we'll both phone. We should get one in a minute over this hill."

The next mile is like an eternity. Finally, a small bar appears on the top of my mobile.

"Stop, here!" I shout.

He pulls over in the next lay-by.

I try you on your mobile while your dad phones your mum back at the house.

"Call the police from there, love. We're struggling with a signal here."

Still there's no reply from you, or your mobile or our house phone.

As we get nearer, your mum sends me a text to say she's got through to the police.

"They're on their way," I sigh. "The police are sending someone over."

"Why would he set this all up with Jez? I don't understand, love." Your dad's brow is furrowed in concentration and stress, sweat is pouring down his temples.

"Will said he needed money for his business. Why didn't he tell me?"

"The stupid lad ... he could have ... Mother and me ...

we would have given him all the money he needed." Your father shakes his head, his eyes are full of tears, yet he keeps them pinned to the winding road.

Again, I try your mobile … no answer. I try Louise … but even she isn't picking up. No one is picking up! I text you, I text Louise, but there is no response. My stomach is in knots. Your father continues to ask his questions.

"Why? The stupid lad! I know he was down. Why wouldn't he talk to us? Why wouldn't he talk to you, Karen?"

"I don't know," I whisper as I shake my head. "All this time I just thought he blamed me, I thought he hated me. All this time he'd set up the whole thing with Jez just for money."

Your dad speeds round another bend in the road. I'm surprised we're not pulled over by the police.

We are back at home within about twenty-five minutes, but it feels like an age. The tyres screech and slide on the gravel drive. The house lights are out and there is zero street lighting.

"Let me go in first, love." Your dad is now calmer, trying to be more in control now we have arrived.

"No … No … we'll do this together."

I can hear sirens, but they seem like they are miles away. You have bolted the front door. We can just about see you through the glass panels, lying still on the hallway floor.

Your dad screams through the letterbox, all sense of calm disappearing, "Will! Will! Let us in. Wake up, son. Let us in, please!"

I run to the garage, knowing there's a spare back door key in there somewhere, but I can't open the door, the battery's dead on my fob.

31

Will

Saturday Night 10pm

The sky is deep blue and the rays make my eyes stream; it's a struggle to keep them open. Sharp grains of sand whip the side of my face and my limbs are contorted in an odd position. Weirdly, my left side is numbed cold and stone-like, whilst my right side swelters in this mid-day sun. I seriously need painkillers and my head is splitting. It's too late in the day for a hangover.

Gulls squeal like sirens and lightning streaks across the sky, which only adds to my confusion. What's happening?

In the pit of my stomach there's a feeling of impending doom.

I call you for some tablets but you're all chasing the waves and totally oblivious. Your screams pierce through me, increasing my pain. There's a tall, dark shadow behind you. You're arguing. I rub my eyes to focus. You look like you're being dragged away by some random stranger. There's nothing I can do. He has you, he has them, and he has a gun!

"Shit, it's him... Karen! Get away from my kids... Run, Karen!" I try to scream but instead it's a muffled slur that babbles from my mouth.

"You sick bastard, leave them alone!" Again, I try, but only confused garble leaves my lips.

Then, there's voices, from nowhere:

"Will, baby, stay with me."

"Son, wake up."

"Dad?... Stop shaking me, you're making my head worse."

The loud voices rip through me. I clamp my temples with my fists to try to control this agony.

The sky still flashes blue. The sirens keep screeching. My head is excruciating. My family are dragged away.

32

Karen

Saturday night 11pm

The police arrive within minutes, yet it seems like an eternity. Your dad is guided away by one of the officers from where he has been hammering on the door with his fists. His shoulders are heaving whilst he sobs.

"Let us deal with this, please sir," the officer says gently.

"The garage," I try to explain through my tears. "Will always leaves a spare backdoor key in the garage."

Without the fob working, the garage door won't open with my force alone, but together we all manage prize it open, and it lets out a huge groaning creak, the hinges rusty with age. I race in and grab the backdoor key from its hook by the workbench.

Your dad is straight back to the letterbox, helplessly watching and pleading to his son motionless on the floor. "Will, Will, please son, it's Dad. Wake up, Will lad, please."

The officer is opening the backdoor of the house and the lights come on. I'm directly behind and rush towards you, shaking you, screaming your name.

Your dad is in the house now, and he too is trying to shake you, yelling at you, "Come on son, wake up." He's in bits, hysterical.

"Will baby, stay with me," I plead.

We are both dragged away. They say there's a faint pulse and they work on you for the longest few moments of my life. The officer tries in vain to resuscitate you but it's no good. We are too late. Your face drains of any remaining colour and you are cold, you are gone. You lie there, motionless. Between us, we hold you, willing you to wake. But there's no breathing, no movement, no response. Your frown lines have disappeared—you are at peace.

33

Monday one week later

Why, Will? Why? Things weren't that bad, Christ knows. If we had to go bankrupt, there's no shame in that, but to organise a burglary, with Jez of all people. For God's sake, why?

All that time you made me feel like it was my fault: my bid, my log cabin. I just thought you were depressed, I thought you hated me. Why didn't you say? Why didn't you explain to me? I never wanted all those things, you know that. I just wanted us to be happy, together, like we used to be.

Why did you do this to us? We used to talk about everything. You could have told me about the business. All this time you had me thinking you were having an affair. I just wish we could go back, keep things simple this time. But your decision was made. You must have mulled it over and over. In your opinion, you were of no use to anyone anymore. No use to me, no use to the girls, no use to your parents. The business was gone. In your opinion, we were better off without you.

We found out that you were in your office the night before we left, and with several whiskeys put pen to paper. Three attempts it took to get the wording right—I'd found the remnants in the bin with two empty bottles when it was all over. You didn't want me to blame myself, but also didn't want me to hate you and your reasons for doing it. If we'd carried on, we would certainly have lost the house and all that we had worked for. You knew if I didn't tell the police and it was a convincing accident that I would still get the life insurance to pay for the house and the business. I'm guessing this was your final act of love—or was it?

Now I have two young girls to bring up on my own with no father; no one to teach them to drive, no one to walk them down the aisle. How the hell do I explain this to two little girls who still have nightmares? One day they'll find out for themselves that the night they saved their daddy's life was all set up by you, just for money. What a total waste of a life! We will never get over this, let alone our attack.

So as I was packing to go to Wales, you knew my toiletry bag was a safe place, that I wouldn't use it until bedtime, that your note was safely tucked away in that side pocket. You clung on to me tight before I left, and the girls. I should have guessed something was wrong, but instead I thought we'd turned a corner. I thought that things might start to get better.

"Have a great time, love you," you'd said. I was convinced that you just wanted some space, hoped that you might be on the mend.

I have so many questions. Why? Why did you not have counselling? Why leave us behind? I can't help it but I hate you right now.

You must have set about your plan within a few hours of us going. The doctors gave you antidepressants. They always made you slightly groggy, and I suppose with the help of a few whiskeys… If you did do it soon after I had

217

gone, then the alcohol would be out of your system, I'm guessing, by the time we were supposed to find you. You sent your last text late enough though; you knew I wouldn't have my phone on in the car. I'm guessing you put on your prosthetic limb at the top of the stairs—perfect.

I always hated those stairs. They were a death trap from day one with that stone floor to fall on. You would get the result you required. I can't quite work out what you did with the bottle of tablets. They weren't found on you. Maybe you just had a handful of pills, but they estimated about forty or so plus several whiskeys. God, you must have felt really out of it. The limb wasn't easy to walk on anyway. I guess you fell from the top of the stairs or threw yourself down them, your head smashing on the stone floor. Gone.

I never thought that at my age I'd be sat here a widow with two young girls, talking to your coffin, with you dressed in your tuxedo, the same tux you wore to the charity do, looking relaxed and so damn handsome. And yet here I am, telling you your story, our story...

So now what do we do?

About the author

Christina Delmonte has worked in Art and Design for thirty years.

She was born in Southampton and now lives in Cheshire with her husband and two children. This is her debut novel.

Lightning Source UK Ltd.
Milton Keynes UK
UKHW011920130721
387112UK00001B/35